When the Summer People Have Gone

When the Summer People Have Gone

Julie Ellis

G.K. Hall & Co. • Chivers Press
Thorndike, Maine USA   Bath, England

This Large Print edition is published by G.K. Hall & Co., USA
and by Chivers Press, England.

Published in 1999 in the U.S. by arrangement with Chivers Press Ltd.

Published in 1999 in the U.K. by arrangement with
Severn House Publishers Ltd.

U.S. Hardcover   0-7838-8567-9 (Romance Series Edition)
U.K. Hardcover   0-7540-3753-3 (Chivers Large Print)
U.K. Softcover   0-7540-3754-1 (Camden Large Print)

The text of this Large Print edition is unabridged.
Other aspects of the book may vary from the original edition.

Set in 16 pt. Plantin by Rick Gundberg.

Printed in the United States on permanent paper.

British Library Cataloguing in Publication Data available

Library of Congress Cataloging in Publication Data

Ellis, Julie.
   When the summer people have gone / Julie Ellis.
     p.   cm.
   ISBN 0-7838-8567-9 (lg. print : hc : alk. paper)
   1. Large type books. I. Title.
   [PS3555.L597W48 1999]
   813′.54—dc21   99-18679

When the Summer People Have Gone

ONE

By the first of December Montauk, New York, had assumed its gaunt winter garb. For a little while, in the summer months, it had radiated an exciting, convivial aura, like a plain woman who has blossomed for a night at a fancy ball. The summer visitors were gone. Second-home owners — except for the most hardy — had closed up their houses for the season, to emerge with fresh vitality over the next Memorial Day weekend. Most motels were boarded up against the harsh winter weather. Some shops were closed, and those still open would schedule vacations during the next three months. Montauk belonged to the 'locals'. Stephanie Richards looked forward each year to this respite.

Most were grateful that the 'Hampton glamour' was in eclipse until the end of May, though they were aware that it was the tourist trade that supported the economy. Senior citizens who could afford it became 'snowbirds', bound for Florida for as many of the winter months as they could manage. Those who couldn't kept themselves occupied with church, volunteer work and the Senior Center.

The youngest of the four Bertonelli children, Stephanie was the only one born in Montauk. Even after twenty-eight years of operating first a pizza parlor and now an 'Italian' restaurant some twenty miles below, the Bertonellis were still newcomers in the eyes of sixth-generation families.

Within her own family Stephanie — Stephie to all who knew her — often felt herself an outsider, except with Grandma Bertonelli, whom she adored. Her long, silken hair, the color of fresh honey and her expressive blue eyes set her apart from the dark-haired, dark-eyed, olive-skinned members of the family, along with her quiet, introspective approach to life and her passion for reading. In high-spirited moments her father, Tony, insisted she was a changeling. Grandma said she was a throwback to an earlier century.

On this gray, bone-chilling morning Stephie parked her nine-year-old Dodge in the driveway of her small Cape Cod home after delivering Lisa, her four-year-old daughter, to her child care provider. Though she was not working this morning, she knew not to cut back on the hours — another mother would instantly grab at replacing Lisa on a full-time basis. Lisa looked forward to this play time, she reassured herself, feeling a guilty pleasure at having a day that belonged to herself alone.

Emerging from the car, she heard the raucous shriek of the telephone. Frowning, she rushed to respond, picked up on the fifth ring, just beating out the answering machine. "Hello —" Breathless from the dash from car to house.

"Stephie, I've just spoken with Tom's attorney . . ." A wariness in her attorney's voice warned her of fresh complications.

"Yes?" For almost two years she'd been fighting for a divorce. *Why is it so easy to get married, and so hard to get divorced?*

"Tom's willing to accept a $9,000 settlement." More than his share of their equity in the house, but Grandma was secretly prepared to provide this ransom. Originally he'd demanded $25,000. Now she was conscious of a pregnant pause. "But he's insisting on joint custody. That you have Lisa on alternate days."

"Is he insane?" Shock blended with rage in her. Half a dozen times in the last two years she'd allowed him to have Lisa overnight, when he was living at home with his aunt. Then his Aunt Alice threw him out, and two months ago he had moved into a rundown motel unit that was officially closed for the season. She'd agreed to his having Lisa on a Saturday night, with his promise to bring her back in time for breakfast on Sunday.

She felt sick as she remembered what Lisa had said when Tom brought her home. *'Mommie, what was Daddy doing with that lady on the other bed? He was bouncing up and down on her — and they had no clothes on.'* She recoiled, hearing in recall Tom's explanation. *'Hey, I thought the kid was asleep.'* Without understanding, Lisa had been upset.

"I know, we brought out at the last hearing that he'd allowed her to witness a sexual encounter." The attorney's voice brought her back to the moment.

Stephie took a deep breath, ordering herself to remain calm. "Joint custody has been ruled out. He can see Lisa at the house — in my presence. He agreed to that!"

"He's done a switch," the attorney said tiredly. "He's signed the papers but a joint custody clause has been added."

"No deal," she rejected. "He'll never see her alone again."

"I'll talk to his attorney," Allen promised.

More lawyer's fees. I can't believe the thousands Grandma has laid out already.

The family didn't know how much this divorce fight had cost so far. They'd be horrified. Horrified, she thought wryly as she walked into the kitchen, that Grandma was spending so much on *her*. It was understood when Grandma went — and please God, don't let that happen for a long, long time — that the restaurant and the house would go to Mom and Dad and the rest divided among the other three children and grandchildren. Everybody knew about the property Grandma owned, bought years ago when everything was dirt cheap.

Was she doing wrong in breaking up her own small family? But what other way was there to go? Almost from the first months of her pregnancy Tom had verbally abused her, humiliated her in public with noisy bursts of temper. So many times she wished she'd fall through the ground when he went on like that. But when he beat her two years ago while Lisa had stood screaming in her crib she'd realised that she and Lisa couldn't live with him. She'd packed up his gear when he was away at work — only during the first few months of their marriage did he hold a steady job — and when he returned that night, she told him they were through.

Almost immediately she knew he was glad to split up. He hated being tied down to a wife. He wanted to carouse at night with his buddies, most of whom were divorced. The whole town knew that the wife of one of them was regularly abused by him. She'd suspected for a long time that Tom had thought he was marrying into money because Grandma owned a successful restaurant. He forgot about the big mortgage payments that had to be met every month until it was paid off six years from now. He forgot that there was a staff to be paid every week, not just in the season but year round. He couldn't believe there were winter weeks when the restaurant operated at a loss.

Tom had been so sure that Grandma — or Mom and Dad — would give them a house as a wedding present. Instead, they'd moved into a house Grandma had owned for years and taken on a huge mortgage. It upset her that there were months when they couldn't meet the mortgage payments. Grandma let it slide but she'd felt awful when she and Tom couldn't meet this obligation.

She washed the few breakfast dishes and dropped into one of the two chairs that flanked the oak dining room table. Why had she married Tom? Sure, he'd oozed charm in those days and she couldn't have known that he'd never hold a permanent job, just drift from one to another. Like his buddies.

I married Tom to get out of the family house. I wasn't a child anymore, I was suffocating at living like one. In towns like this how else do young people escape from family? You live 'at home' until you get married. Only then do you become a grown-up.

She gazed into space without seeing, her mind rerunning thoughts that dogged her through the years. Dad was born in a village in southern Italy; Mom was born in this country. Grandma and Grandpa, she vaguely recalled, had brought Dad to this country when he was three years old. So why did Mom and Dad live the way they would in that village in Italy?

The day after tomorrow Mom and Dad would leave to spend three weeks in Florida with Dad's brother and his wife. Mom waited all year for these three weeks. It was as though Dad was conferring a huge favor. Mom deserved these three weeks — and more. While Mom and Dad were away, Vinnie would take over. Dad never admitted she did more of the managing than Vinnie.

There had been times when she was growing up and saw her father use her mother as his whipping post that she'd asked herself, *'Why does Mom stand for that? Why doesn't she leave him?'* But she knew the reason. In Mom's thinking a man in the house was the symbol of security.

Didn't Mom realise she worked just as hard as Dad did? Dad still thought like the people back in that village where he was born. Grandma didn't think like that, but she was silent to keep peace in the family. To keep the family intact. She went to church every Sunday and prayed for that.

The whole family was upset when she went to Mr Allen to talk about divorcing Tom. To them divorce was a disgrace. Only Grandma understood. And now, she thought with fresh rage, Tom dared to talk about joint custody. After that Saturday night when Lisa stayed with him in his motel room and saw what no four-year-old should see.

No joint custody. That will never happen. Even if I have to pack up and leave town in the middle of the night.

TWO

The morning was a magnificent seascape in gray, Paul Hamilton thought, as he stood on the wrap-around deck of his borrowed house in Montauk and watched the waves pound against the sand below. Not a soul on the beach. Far out on the horizon he saw a lone fishing boat. The steel of the sky reflected on the expanse of ocean. The stillness unbroken except for the occasional plaintive *caw* of a seagull.

The staff at Gorman, Tremont & Ashford Investments Inc — headed by his father-in-law, Ted Gorman — thought he was recuperating from his nasty bout of pneumonia at a posh resort hotel in the Caribbean. Only Emily and her father knew he was holed up here in this house that belonged to Emily's aunt, off somewhere in the Greek Isles. Her father held the keys and kept in touch with the watchman who oversaw the place the nine months in the year when her aunt was not in residence.

His mind shot back to the night he'd come home from the hospital. Emily had been so scared, even though Dr Anderson insisted he was on the road to recovery. He'd never been

14

sick in the eight years they'd been married. Not a day in his life until this. But he'd been exhausted from the frenzied years of twenty-hour days at the office, run down.

He'd spent two weeks recuperating in the apartment, reveling in the extra time he could spend with Mark and Larry. And when his father-in-law suggested he take off another three weeks — *'Go away and get back to your old self'* — he'd grabbed at the excuse to delay his return to the office. But to Emily and her father it was inconceivable that he'd want to spend these three weeks at Montauk . . .

"Paul, for the time it takes you to drive out to Montauk you can fly down to St John's or Martinique!" She stared at him as though convinced he'd lost his mind.

"I need that winter quiet out at Montauk, I can unwind there."

"It won't just be quiet," she protested. "It'll be deserted this time of year. Practically everything will be closed up."

"Honey, people live in Montauk year-round." He tried to sound amused. "I'll stay at your aunt's house — she won't mind."

A small, modern masterpiece that looked down on the Atlantic. That welcomed the outdoors within its walls. A vast expanse of beach where he could walk in blessed solitude. "Talk to your father about my staying there." He struggled to sound matter-of-fact, but he longed for this escape. "I'll be back in time to spend Christmas with you and the kids. And to be there for the office madness," he added with an ironic smile. The Christmas party was a ritual his father-in-law cherished.

Emily sighed.

"I'll talk to Dad, but I'll bet you'll be back in town in three days."

Last summer he and Emily and the kids had spent two weeks out here at the height of the season. Emily's aunt Jean was the only family member with whom she felt some closeness, though for the kids' sake she pretended devotion to her father. *'Let them have one grandparent in their lives. They see my mother once a year, she's a stranger to them.'* Their step-grandmother was four years older than Emily. God, he wished his parents had lived to see Mark and Larry. They would have been such warm, loving grand-parents.

These two weeks out here he'd made a habit of rising very early, while Emily and the boys slept, walked on the still deserted beach, which would be a sea of bodies in another two hours. He'd gone for breakfast at the Sea Breeze or Bird-on-the-Roof, both with only a sprinkling of patrons at this early hour but with lines waiting an hour later. In a corner of his mind he'd imagined the wonderful serenity of being out here when the summer people had gone. What a contrast to the insanity of the trading floor of the firm!

Even in the hectic summer season he'd been intrigued by the small town. The business structures — most of them in the Tudor style introduced by Carl Fisher, the entrepreneur who'd built Miami — were one or two stories in height, except for what was known as the Tower. Located at the traffic circle, this rose to an impressive seven stories. A charming old-world gazebo, constructed just a few years ago, graced the Village Green.

Probably at Christmas, so close at hand, the town would erupt into a spectacular holiday display. Emily said her aunt lovingly referred to Montauk as the 'special Hampton' where people lived quiet, placid lives with no concern for the celebrities who inhabited the other Hamptons.

He grimaced, visualising the madness at the firm at the approach of Christmas. He hated the Christmas party, where everybody made a pretense of enjoying themselves when in truth, the major thought pervading every mind was, 'How big a bonus check will I get this year?' Bonuses that would be delivered not at Christmas time but early in the new year. Bonuses that could far exceed yearly earnings.

Christmas had been fun at the high school where he'd taught all too briefly. The kids had looked forward to it with such fervor. He could hear in his mind how one student had described it: *'Hey man, it means presents! It means vacation time! What can beat that?'*

How had he allowed himself to be enticed

away from teaching? He'd loved it. He'd felt he was doing something worthwhile with his life. Why had he allowed Emily's father to push him first into going back for an MBA, then coming into the firm?

But he'd felt compelled to follow that course. He'd known from their first meeting that Ted Gorman was disappointed in Emily's choice of a husband. Her father hoped for a son-in-law from a wealthy family, with the contacts this would provide. Then Emily got pregnant and the two of them were so happy. But all the more reason to listen to his father-in-law's urging. They were living in a tiny one-bedroom apartment in the Gramercy Park area. It had been a studio apartment that the management divided into a one-bedroom.

'Paul, we have to get out of here. There's no room for a crib, a carriage — all the equipment we'll need when the baby comes!'

They were going to be a family and Emily was ecstatic. Her mother and father had divorced when she was seven. Until she was thirteen she commuted between her father's household and her mother's, then at thirteen she was shipped off to boarding school. No room in her parents' lives for a daughter. Nannies and boarding school had been stand-ins for her mother and father. She vowed that would never happen to their children.

Her father was now in his third marriage, her mother drifting from man to man, being dried

18

out at posh rehab clinics at regular intervals.

Emily's father came up with the down-payment on a four-bedroom, two-bath condo on West End Avenue. Neither he nor Emily considered a move to suburbia. He secretly suspected that Ted Gorman's pride prompted his gift. How would it look to his friends if his daughter lived in 'middle-class squalor'?

Emily planned to work up until the last minute at her job, which she loved and which held potential for big salary increases, and to return after three months' maternity leave. But with the condo came a huge monthly maintenance and with a baby they needed a nanny, neither of which could be handled on the salary of a third-year high school teacher and fledgling publicist. Paul had managed to earn his MBA in a year and a half and had gone straight into the training program at the firm.

In his sedated mind during those days in the hospital he'd welcomed not being on the trading floor. He hated their whole lifestyle. So little time with the kids, no social life. They'd lost touch with old friends. He was an English teacher who loved books, but the favorite reading matter of his crew of associates at the firm was *Soldier of Fortune* and *Guns and Ammo*.

Don't think about three weeks from now, he exhorted himself. Enjoy each hour out here. As always Emily had proved herself totally efficient. She'd contacted the caretaker, arranged for the thermostat to be raised from the non-occupancy fifty degrees to a comfortable seventy-two, the hot water turned on, and logs delivered for the two fireplaces, one in the living room, the other in the master bedroom. The phone was connected, along with cable TV. *Emily is so efficient, so bright. Why can't she understand what the job does to me?*

Emily had worried that he'd insisted on driving up last night in a thunderstorm. But the rain had stopped by the time he swung off the Long Island Expressway at Exit 70. Once on Route 27 he'd felt the winter serenity as he drove along the main streets of Bridgehampton, Wainscott, Easthampton and Amagansett. Arriving in Montauk he'd felt an odd sense of coming home.

He'd phoned and talked to Emily. Mark and Larry were asleep. Then he'd started a fire in the bedroom fireplace and drifted off to sleep before the mesmerizing blaze. Two hours later he'd awakened and transferred himself to the queen-sized sleigh bed. The symphony of the waves caressing the sand a bedtime lullaby that coaxed him into slumber again.

Go down to the beach, he ordered himself, abandoning introspection. Walk for a while, then drive into town for supplies. There was coffee in the house plus sugar and salt but nothing else except exotic canned items bought last summer at Ocean View, the local gourmet shop.

He zipped up his gray down jacket, reached

into a pocket for the knit cap he'd stashed there earlier and pulled it over his dark hair, grown far beyond the length approved by Wall Street traders. He left the house and walked down to the pristine sand, untouched by footprints or four-wheel-drive car tracks.

Relishing the brisk cold of the morning, he walked with unexpected vigor. Not another human being ahead of him. The sand was untrampled at this early hour. The boarded-up motel units exuded a poignant aura, as though mourning their lack of guests.

The blissful quiet was all at once splintered by the deep bark of a dog. He turned to face a playful — and huge — Bernese.

"Hi there, old boy —" He paused to provide the expected byplay.

"Old girl," a light feminine voice corrected. "Her name is Chloe."

He smiled at the small, slim young woman who strolled beside him now.

"My apologies," he said. "Chloe's a great dog." He chuckled because Chloe was demanding more attention. "She's still a pup, isn't she?"

"I think so. Oh, she isn't mine, she belongs to one of the store owners on Main Street. I run into her often." Affection in her voice. "Like me, she loves the winter beach."

"So do I. It's magical."

"It forever astonishes me that so few people come down here in winter. But secretly I'm glad." Her smile was whimsical. "I pretend it belongs to me alone."

"Do you live here year-round?" He felt strangely drawn to her.

"I was born here —" She reached for a stick, tossed it for Chloe. "I think it's one of the most beautiful spots in the world. I love the ocean. It's never the same, a little different each day. I love to fall asleep to the sound of the waves coming in to the shore. Sometimes a sweet lullaby, sometimes a thunderous opera. But always wonderful."

"It's so different now from the summer season." She would wait impatiently for the summers to end, he thought in a corner of his mind. Dreaming of days like this.

"Have you just moved to Montauk?" He felt curiosity welling in her.

"I'm staying in a borrowed house for three weeks. It belongs to my wife's aunt. She spends summers out here. I've just got over a bad case of pneumonia, and the doctor said, 'Go somewhere and rest up'."

Her eyes lit with laughter. "He thought you'd go to Florida or the Caribbean and soak up sun," she guessed. "But you chose Montauk —" A softness in her voice said, 'You made the right choice.'

"Where better to relax?" It was as though they shared a secret. "I was out here last July for two weeks. It was fine, but I could imagine it off-season, with the summer people gone, the beach deserted. I knew I wanted to come back here one winter day."

"Whenever I have a serious problem, I come down here and walk. Some people go to church. I suppose this is my church." A tilt of her head asked, 'Do you agree with me?' "I know that people talk about the Hamptons as the 'in' place to be, and Montauk is part of the town of East Hampton. But Montauk is a world apart from the rest of the Hamptons, except for the weeks between Memorial Day and Labor Day."

He hesitated, feeling a compulsion to linger with her. It was as though he'd suddenly moved into another world. "Would you like to go somewhere for coffee and talk about the wonders of Montauk?"

She paused, seeming in inner debate. "I'm in the midst of getting a divorce. I don't think my lawyer would want me to walk into a coffee shop, where probably everybody will know me, with a strange man," she said with candor and wistful regret. "My almost-ex is vindictive. He's been making life rough for me and my lawyer. But thanks."

"If you can drink coffee black, we could have it on the deck of my borrowed house," he coaxed impulsively. "Fresh-ground beans . . ."

"I'd like that," she said with an air of quiet pleasure. "And I promise to tell you all about Montauk."

THREE

"My house is back there," he pointed in the opposite direction. "Oh, isn't it about time we introduced ourselves?" *He has such an attractive smile.* "I'm Paul Hamilton."

"I'm Stephanie Richards. Everybody calls me Stephie."

Chloe was deserting them to join a pair of black Labradors who were sauntering into view.

"More beach lovers," Paul said, chuckling. "The four-footed population is smarter than mere humans."

All at once the sun broke through a cluster of clouds, spilling a swathe of gold across the sand.

"Oh, the weather people were wrong! It's going to be a glorious day." Stephie glowed. "But I like the gray days, too. The earth just changes its dress." She gazed at him in speculation. "What's your favorite time of year?"

"Every season except summer," he said wryly. "Summers in Manhattan are ghastly."

"Summers out here are frantic. But you know that. Thank God for all the Irish students who come over to work in the Hamptons during school vacations —" She giggled. "And to party."

"We talked with the Irish waitresses at the Sea Breeze when we were out here," he recalled. "I have a buddy who earned his PhD at Trinity in Dublin."

"We all kind of look forward to their arrival — most of them," she conceded. "We had one girl at our restaurant last year who could never wake up in time for the breakfast shift — not after partying till five A.M. My father switched her to working the dinner shift, from five to ten P.M." He felt a churning restlessness in her. "I've never been further from Montauk than New York City. Oh, once I went with my grandmother to visit cousins in Boston. But you know," she said thoughtfully, "I'm always glad to be back home again."

"There's the house." He pointed to a sprawling multi-glassed, white-brick contemporary that she knew by sight only. "It's sad to think of all the lovely houses out here that are closed up for most of the year."

"I often think that." She'd never said as much to anyone else. "They sit there with their windows and sliders boarded up and wait to come alive again. It's sad, too, to see all the empty houses in a world where there are so many homeless. We don't see that here in town," she conceded, "but we read about it in the newspapers and see it on television. And there are all the young couples here who get married and have such an awful time finding a place to live. If they rent, it's usually for nine months of the year, and then they have to search around for some place to stay during the summer months.”

“Not much of a supply,” he surmised, “and what there is I’ll bet is expensive.”

“A few manage to buy a ‘fixer-upper’. Tom and I were lucky. My grandmother owned this little house that we bought with a big, big mortgage . . .” She grew somber. “Tom’s my almost-ex.”

“I know about big mortgages,” he commiserated. “We have a whopper.” He grinned, stared upward at the house. “Prepare for a climb, Stephie!”

She felt a surge of self-consciousness. *What am I doing, having coffee with a man I just met a few minutes ago? At his house.* But it seemed so right.

“You’ve got to see the view from the deck.” He seemed to sense her unease. “It’s fabulous. I’ll bring out a couple of chairs for us before I put up the coffee.” *He understands.*

She walked beside him up the wide stairs that led to the wrap-around deck, paused to gaze out at the fishing boat far off on the horizon. *This is just a casual encounter between two people who love this beach. And he wants to talk about Montauk. I told him I’ve lived here all my life.*

He brought out two colorfully-cushioned redwood chaises and positioned them for a perfect view of the Atlantic.

“Coffee’s coming up,” he said. “I’ll expect a travelogue to go with it. Wow, was I impressed by the signs I read coming out — I hadn’t noticed them on the earlier trip. Bridge-hampton, settled 1656. Amagansett, settled 1680. And the sign just outside of Montauk that reminds tourists to 'Visit Historic Montauk Lighthouse and Museum'." His eyes were reminiscent. "I took Mark and Larry, my two kids, to see it." He chuckled. "They were so impressed."

"Oh, everybody wants to see the Montauk Lighthouse. In 1790 President Washington approved a Congressional order to build it. The tower's one hundred feet tall and now, after all these years, with the ocean eating away at its base, the lighthouse sits almost at the edge of the cliff. And, you know the new movie, *Amistad*, that we keep hearing about?"

Paul nodded. "The one that deals with slave trading back in the early 1800s."

"The *Amistad* came up from Cuba and anchored in Fort Pond Bay here in Montauk. By then the Africans had revolted and taken over the ship and the leader, a man named Cinque, left the *Amistad* to come ashore in a small boat. That's when the crew of a revenue cutter captured them."

"Oh, this town must be loaded with history." Paul radiated enthusiasm as he headed back into the house.

"I'll be your tour guide," she picked up his mood, and all at once was aware of color rising in her face. Did that sound as though she meant to show him the town?

I won't stay long. I'll go back to the car, drive over

to see Grandma. She'll be so upset when she hears about Tom's latest craziness. She keeps telling me it's all right, she'll handle the lawyer's fees, but he bills me even for a five-minute call. Divorce is an insidious plot dreamt up by lawyers. For them it's a pot of gold.

Paul had left a slider slightly ajar. The pungent aroma of coffee beans being ground filtered out to her. Tom had scoffed at her when she'd bought a coffee grinder. *'You've got money to waste on crap like that?'*

She worked hard — usually at two jobs — while Tom floated from one job to another, always complaining about his bosses. He didn't want to work. He liked being laid off, being between jobs for weeks at a time.

Since she'd thrown him out of the house, he'd sponged on his aunt. Grandma thought he'd grab at that $9,000 Mr Allen dangled before him and take off for some other town. Why was he plaguing her with a demand for joint custody? He didn't want that responsibility.

Was it because somebody had told him about Gary taking her to dinner once every week or so? He could mess around all he wanted but he was furious that she might be going out with somebody. She knew Gary wanted to marry her once she was free. Gary was a kind, gentle man who'd be a real father to Lisa. But she wasn't ready to make another commitment. She wasn't free to do that.

"Coffee coming up." Paul's exuberant announcement punctured her introspection.

He brought a small table, topped by a pair of oversized mugs, onto the deck and deposited it between the pair of chaises.

"You aren't cold out here, are you?" he asked solicitously.

"No, I'm fine. The sun is wonderful."

"When I was a kid," he reminisced, "we had a second home in northern New Jersey. I remember sitting out on our porch in a sheltered corner and feeling the sun burning my skin when the temperature was ten degrees below zero." His face grew serious. "My parents died within six months of each other — from lung cancer. They were both heavy smokers." He paused. "They'd wanted me to be a teacher, like themselves."

Stephie's face was luminous. "You're a teacher?"

"I was for three years." *Why does he look so pained?* "I loved it. I taught in what was known as a 'bad school'. Drugs, guns, gangs — everything bad about urban schools was part of the scene. But it was a challenge to me. I knew how those kids had to fight for survival. I felt I was reaching out to them." His face was taut. "I connected with my kids. I related to them and they knew it. And then I walked out on them."

"You gave them three years —" *He cares about people. He shouldn't be hurting this way.*

"My parents taught for thirty years. They always felt that teaching was a way of giving back to their community. They were never rich but they felt they'd been given a comfortable life. Far better than the lives of so many others in the city. I left teaching after three years for a job that paid me four times my teaching salary."

"All through high school I dreamt about becoming a teacher," she said softly after a moment. "But my parents needed me in the restaurant. Nobody in our family ever went to college. Even my grandmother, who's always on my side, said there are too few teaching jobs out here to bother trying for one. I think she was scared I'd get my teaching certificate and take off. We're a close family."

"I was an only child," he told her. "Like both my parents. But we were a tightly knit family. And every night," he said passionately, "I curse the tobacco industry for bringing premature death to so many good people."

"What do you do now?" *How sad that a dedicated teacher had been lost.*

"I sell derivatives for an investment banking firm." His voice was riddled with contempt.

She frowned in bewilderment. "I don't know what that is . . ."

"It's a job where very young people make very much money — if they can hack it. A derivative is an *option* to buy or sell something in the future, or an *obligation* to do this. A successful derivatives salesperson is a con artist. My father-in-law makes millions every year. He expects me to be doing that in another five years." He chuckled at her stare of astonishment. "Not only baseball players and movie stars make that kind of money. It happens regularly on the financial scene."

"Can't you go back to teaching?" *Does he truly need to make all that money? Teaching doesn't pay minimum wages.*

He responded as though reading her mind. "We have a huge mortgage, hefty monthly maintenance payments on our co-op, and two sons who're a long way from college — Mark is six and Larry four — but the pundits keep telling us now is the time to plan."

"Lisa will go to college some day," she said with fierce determination. "I figure there're state schools and college loans and —" She gestured her inability to plot that far ahead.

Right now my main concern is to get my divorce, manage to survive as a single mother. Lots of women are doing that these days. But I won't go back home.

"Tell me about Montauk," Paul coaxed, intent, she sensed, on dispelling this somber mood. "What's that tall building in the center of town? Tall, that is," he said, chuckling, "for Montauk. I heard someone refer to it as the Tower."

"That's our Tower," she said and laughed. "Co-op apartments now. It was built back in the 1920s as an office building, when Carl Fisher came here with wild ideas about making Montauk the Miami of the north. But the Wall Street crash of '29 put a stop to that."

31

"Thank God." Paul shuddered. "All this would be lost to us."

She felt a surge of pleasure that he shared her feelings.

"Montauk used to be an island, oh, about 15,000 years ago. It's older, geologically, than the rest of Long Island. In 1684 the English bought 31,000 acres from the Montauk Indians, land that extended from the eastern end of Southampton up to Hither Hills in Montauk."

"Bought it for next to nothing," he guessed.

"For twenty coats, twenty-four each of knives, hoes, hatchets and looking glasses plus one hundred of a tool called a mux."

"What is a mux?" Paul asked good-humoredly.

"The Indians used them to drill holes in clam shells, to be strung to make wampum. Back in those days," she said whimsically, "Montauk was pasture land for sheep and cattle from further down the island. Then in 1686 settlers bought 10,000 acres beyond Hither Hills from the Montauk Indians for £100."

What is happening to me? Why am I so drawn to this man I've just met? We live in different worlds, come from different worlds.

She drained her coffee mug, rose awkwardly to her feet. "Thanks so much for the coffee. I have to run. I have a million things to do this morning."

"I'm glad Chloe brought us together." He was on his feet now. "It's been great talking with

32

you —" His eyes told her he wanted to continue this encounter.

"Enjoy your stay in town and thanks for the coffee." She sought refuge in an impersonal facade. "Bye now!" An effort of lightness that she didn't feel.

She left him standing on the deck and hurried down to the beach, knowing that his gaze followed her. Drive over to Grandma's, she ordered herself. Tell her about this latest craziness of Tom's.

FOUR

The windows in the large Bertonelli kitchen, modernized far beyond the other rooms of the sixty-seven-year-old house, were steamed over as the cozy warmth of the indoors clashed with the increasing outdoor chill. Once again the morning sun was in retreat. Tina Bertonelli frowned as she placed more chunks of wood in the Franklin stove. Her small, rounded sixty-eight-year-old body reflected little of the hard years of raising four children while she strived alongside her late husband to build a successful, small-town restaurant. She seemed to be digesting the report her favorite grandchild had just dumped on her.

"You can't let Tom have joint custody." She sat at the table with Stephie again. "Make Mr Allen understand that."

"What made Tom suddenly ask for joint custody?" But before her grandmother could reply, she supplied the answer herself. "He's sore because somebody told him I was seeing Gary. He can't stand that. So once a week I go out with Gary for dinner — it's nothing serious. Not that it's any of Tom's business," she flared.

"Stephie, everybody in town knows Gary's

mad about you," Tina chided indulgently. "They know he's just waiting for your divorce to come through so he can pop the question."

"Grandma, I don't want to think about getting married again. I told Gary on Saturday night we can't see each other again until the divorce papers are signed."

She did think about Gary, her mind reproached. He was a good man, gentle, hardworking and he loved kids. Though she hadn't seen much of him, Lisa liked Gary. He'd be a good father. And it was scary to think of the years ahead as a single mother. Instinct told her that the roughest years were yet to come.

But I'm not ready to start a new marriage. I'm not free to do that. Not yet —

Tina rose from the table and crossed to the pair of ovens, the expensive professional type installed years ago to allow her to provide some of the baking for the restaurant. She checked the contents of each and smiled in approval.

"The baking's done for the day," she said briskly. She was in the kitchen each morning before five A.M. to prepare what her oldest son called the restaurant's 'fine baking'. At this time of year there were the additional family needs. Right after Thanksgiving she'd begun to prepare the huge fruitcake that would appear on the much-extended Christmas dinner table. Stephie knew she'd been macerating the candied fruit for the loaves of stollen. Already batches of cookie dough resided in the freezer, designed to please the grandchildren. "Drive with me to make my delivery, then let's go down to the Bridgehampton mall. I need a couple of things at Lechter's. Then we'll go over to Encore and buy some paperbacks." She paused. "Stephie, you're not listening to me."

"Yes, I am." Stephie pulled herself back to the moment. Her mind had wandered to that tiny parcel of time when she'd sat on the deck with Paul Hamilton. He said he had two sons. Without knowing anything about his small family, she was sure he was a great father. He was warm and compassionate. He had loved his students and they'd loved him.

"So?" Tina prodded. "We're going to the mall?"

"Sure. It's my day off. Let's live it up." She contrived a convivial smile. Free time would soon be a rarity. After New Year's, when her midweek hours would be cut short at the restaurant, she'd start working at the supermarket on the midweek days. Weekends she'd work breakfast, lunch and dinner shifts at the restaurant. Lisa would be with Grandma.

"And we'll have lunch out," Tina decreed with a glint in her eyes, and Stephie laughed. Mom and Dad never knew about their secret excursions from time to time to South Fork restaurants. To Grandma these were cherished occasions. "I might even have dessert." She sighed, inspecting her waistline. "But I won't have cream in my coffee."

36

Stephie helped load the trays of baked goods into the family station wagon and took her place up front beside her grandmother, trying to keep her mind from going back to that small interlude with Paul Hamilton. She'd probably never see him again.

From the restaurant they headed south on Route 27 to Bridgehampton Commons, the major mall in the Hamptons. This time of year the traffic was light, in such contrast to the July — August hassle. At the mall they shopped at Lechter's, then headed for Encore, the attractive, sprawling bookshop that Stephie adored.

"My treat," Tina said, in high spirits though Stephie knew that Grandma, too, was anxious about Tom's new demands. "Pick out half a dozen paperbacks — that'll hold you for a while."

They lingered at Encore until Stephie made her choices, headed for the always charming, accommodating clerks at the registers. Grandma handed over her charge plate, exchanging light conversation with their clerk while the transaction was completed, and then they headed for lunch at Razzano's.

Walking into the cozy restaurant Stephie felt herself caressed by its warmth. They were early — there was an abundance of unoccupied tables. Tina walked to a rear table, settled herself in an aura of complacency. Stephie peeled away her jacket, positioned her parcel of paperbacks on the floor and sat down.

Grandma loved eating out, Stephie thought tenderly. Here *she* was being served. For most of her waking hours, for so many years, she was the one who served. The others wouldn't understand what these secret excursions meant to Grandma. Since she was seven she'd been Grandma's partner, even then realising these small, special occasions were not to be shared with the family.

They ordered with playful discussion, then settled back in quiet pleasure.

"You're the only one of the children or the grandchildren who likes to read," Tina said, an oft-repeated analysis after a visit to Encore. "You get that from me. Sometimes I think reading was what saved me from falling apart in bad times." Stephie knew there had been rough periods financially and emotionally. "I suppose it's the same with a lot of people."

The nostalgic glow in her eyes told Stephie she'd talk now about how she'd discovered the pleasures of reading when she was a young girl in a village in Italy in the midst of World War Two. A young American lieutenant had been billeted in her family house when the 7th Army was fighting a desperate battle to push the Nazis out of Italy. Sometimes she suspected that Grandma had been in love with the American lieutenant.

"That lieutenant was a wonderful man," Tina said with quiet intensity. "He smuggled army supplies to us — to other villagers, too — when we were fighting to survive. He brought my mother blankets, and Mama and my sisters and I made them into coats and jackets that we needed so badly. He brought food to us when we were hungry. Some of the people called him *'Mio Dio'*."

Stephie knew about the English language paperbacks that he gave Grandma, and how he'd helped her improve her English. He instilled in her his own love of books. Paul Hamilton loved books, Stephie thought suddenly. Tom had always made nasty cracks about her love for reading. *'Stupid little whore, pretendin' you're somebody!'* Grandma knew the American lieutenant had survived the war because the first Christmas after VE Day the family had received a Christmas card.

Reading saved her sanity, too, Stephie conceded, while part of her mind listened to her grandmother reminiscing about the traumatic years when American GIs were so welcomed by the Italian village. *Grandma loves to talk about those years but she's trying to get my mind off Tom's newest craziness. How do I deal with this? I'm scared. So scared.*

FIVE

Paul decided to linger over his late breakfast at Mr John's Pancake House when his good-humored waitress rushed to refill his empty coffee cup. The aroma of bacon sizzling on the grill, the steamed-over plate-glass window, filled him with a sense of well-being.

The atmosphere was warm and friendly, reminding him of early morning breakfasts at Cosmos on East 23rd Street and Second Avenue, when he and Emily lived in that one-bedroom apartment and he was teaching. Those had been happy times, though they had to budget to meet the car payments and agonized over the costs of dental bills. Why had he and Emily allowed her father to seduce them into the high-flying lifestyle that kept him chained to a job he loathed?

God, it was wonderful to sit here, far removed from the insanity of the trading floor. No sense of rush here, everybody seemed so relaxed. At least, on the surface. Mr John's would be closing shortly, for a month or so. The Sea Breeze and Bird-on-the-Roof had already closed for the season.

He should stop stalling, he reproached himself. Take the car over to the IGA and load up on supplies. And pick up a copy of the *Times*. No, he rejected. No newspapers. Don't even watch the news on television. At least not today. He was here to unwind. He'd packed the half-dozen novels Emily had bought for him. Bring a chaise out on the deck, stretch out in the sun and read until lunch time. On the deck the sun would be warm and inviting, despite the low temperature. That's all he meant to do these three weeks: eat, read, sleep.

He left the restaurant, drove the short distance to the IGA and went inside to shop. He saw a slim figure in a red down jacket, thought for a moment it was Stephie and was oddly disappointed to realize it wasn't. Stephie was warm, charming. Beautiful. He'd been disappointed that she'd dashed off so quickly. He'd felt comfortable — relaxed — talking with her.

He roamed the supermarket's aisles, relishing the ability to disregard the passage of time. At the rear he debated before the deli counter. Choose things for lunch. At the firm, if he bothered with lunch at all, it was a donut or bagel grabbed from the lunch cart that appeared in a designated hall at the appropriate hour.

Emily is so enthralled that her father promises I'll be moved up from associate to a vice-president in another year or so. She knows the odds of an associate being promoted. Most are dumped by the wayside. I'm the Chief's son-in-law. That gives me

41

special privileges. In five years the old man expects me to be a principal. That means close to a million a year. God, those figures are still unreal to me! But if I stay in the business, I'll be in a loony bin by then.

Stephie was awed when I told her I'd taught for three years. She probably thinks I'm a dork for cutting out of that scene. It's her vision of heaven. She said she was getting a divorce. Her husband must be a creep. She mentioned a little girl. It'll be rough to raise a child alone.

A clerk at the deli counter served him. Now he was in a rush to get out of the store and back to the house. *Stop thinking about the firm. For the next three weeks forget it exists.*

At the house he put away the groceries, carried a chaise out to the deck. The sun drenched the area with sensuous warmth. The beach was deserted except for the same pair of Labradors he'd seen earlier, though Chloe was gone. All right, grab a book, settle down and read.

He chose a book at random, reached for the cordless phone, then hung it back in place. No phone calls out here. This wasn't the trading floor. Without discarding his jacket — though moments later he unzipped it because the morning sun felt more like June than December — he settled himself on the chaise, tried to focus on the novel. How long had it been since he had the luxury of reading?

His mind refused to cooperate. He needed to unwind more before he could give himself up to reading. He lay back against the cushioned chaise, closed his eyes, willed himself to relax. He awoke forty minutes later, unexpectedly rested.

He spied a fishing boat close to shore, watched with lazy interest. Late in the season for fishing, he thought, but those aboard seem to be having luck. Dozens of seagulls were fighting for the fish that were being tossed back into the ocean.

Involuntarily his mind shot back to his training period at the firm, the agonizing period of serving as an analyst, the bottom of the pole in investment banking. No less agony when he was promoted — as his connections guaranteed — to associate.

The trading floor at any investment firm was the same, he'd read somewhere — a noisy, nerve-wracking jungle. The floor a maze of wires and cables that brought life to the endless array of necessary equipment. Hundreds of phones, computers, TV monitors, Reuters and Telerate screens. The noise a shock to the uninitiated. Loudspeakers screeching out pertinent information with an air of near-hysteria. To communicate with somebody only a few feet away in that nerve-shattering cacophony the use of a phone was essential. He closed his eyes and re-lived his last battle with Emily, a few weeks before he came down with pneumonia . . .

"How can you talk about leaving the firm?" Emily gaped in disbelief. "You're moving up so fast! Look at the future ahead for you!"

"We have no life! No time for the kids, no time

for each other. And it won't be better for years," he forestalled her stock reply. "I feel like a machine, a robot programmed to deal with clients."

"I work long hours, too," she shot back. "But we manage quality time with Mark and Larry —"

God, he loathed that phrase 'quality time'. He took a deep breath, fought for calm. "You enjoy your work. I hate what I'm doing." He couldn't bring himself to say to Emily, 'Your father's firm has changed through the years. Once it was highly respected, ethical — now it's a sea of sharks, out to screw investors!' Her father had refrained from mentioning to her that seven months ago the firm had been reprimanded by regulators for the way it sold derivatives. What did it matter when he was earning millions?

"Paul, you've become neurotic. Be logical. We have two children to raise. We can't live in a run-down slum, send them to over-crowded public schools where kids come with guns and knives and box-cutters. It's a matter of time . . ." She tried for a softer approach. "We won't always work such hectic hours. We're laying the groundwork for a great future for us and the boys."

"I'm bushed. I'm going to sleep." It was past two A.M. He'd be up in four hours.

How could he expect Emily to understand? They came from two different worlds. His parents were middle-class teachers who budgeted to manage a ten-day trip to Europe once in five years or five days in Bermuda at a spring school break. Emily's father and his third wife owned an eleven-room condo in the East Sixties, a condo in Palm Beach and a house on Nantucket. Her stepmother drove a top of the line Mercedes. Her father was driven to and from the offices in a chauffeur-driven Cadillac limousine complete with bar and television. They spent more on a dinner party than his father earned in a month.

In those years at college, Emily had seemed to want to escape from that glittering world. Sure, after her first year she'd moved from the dorm into a gorgeously furnished co-op sublet. But along with him she'd joined literacy groups, tutored kids in housing projects, worked to raise funds for AIDS victims. *What happened to us since college?*

The shrill ringing of the phone jarred him from introspection. He picked it up. "Hello?"

"Oh —" A young, feminine voice began to giggle. "I guess you're not Vivian."

"No, I'm not," he agreed.

"Sorry." His caller slammed down the receiver.

He was conscious of a chill in the air now. The sun was in retreat. He would go inside, make some coffee, stop feeling so tense. *I'm out here to relax.*

In the spacious kitchen that would do credit to a fine restaurant, he ground some more beans, something there was never time for in the city.

He went through the small ritual and sauntered out across the large dining area into the living room to wait for the final swoosh that would tell him the coffee was ready. Relishing yet again the exquisite quiet in the house.

He dropped into a lounge chair that faced the sliders, drapes drawn wide to provide a view of the water, less vibrantly blue than when he'd arrived from his trek into town. Subconsciously he smiled while Stephie's voice echoed in his head: *'I love the ocean. It's never the same, a little different each day. I love to fall asleep to the sound of the waves coming in to the shore. Sometimes a sweet lullaby, sometimes a thunderous opera.'*

He mused about the kind of student she must have been. School wouldn't have been easy for her. She was cut from a different mold. But she would have been a joy to the right teacher. *Why did I desert teaching? I had something to offer. Those kids needed me — I was making a difference. I failed them.*

Again his mind swung back to the one genuinely serious conversation he'd ever had with Clint Winters. Clint loved being a derivatives salesman. He couldn't understand anybody not loving it. He thought derivatives was the best place in the whole investment banking deal.

"Hey, we're in a money-making machine," Clint chortled. "Where else can anybody our age make the kind of loot we make? Maybe in Hollywood," he shrugged. "Sure, we work long hours but look at the rewards. I can't wait to see my bonus this year." All at once his face hardened. "Of course, if they fuck me, I'll cut out the minute my bonus check clears. But you and I, we're survivors," he said with fresh assurance. "Me because I've got the killer instinct — and you," he grinned knowingly, "you've got the big boy behind you."

"Clint, it doesn't bother you that some of these clients may be ruined for life?"

"Look, they should know they're taking risks. They can make a bundle or be taken to the cleaners. It's a gamble. Hell, life's a gamble."

But too often clients were totally unaware of the hidden risks they were taking. That didn't seem to bother anybody at the firm. The deal was to make as much money as possible and to hell with who got hurt. But he felt sick when he realized how they were screwing their clients.

And in three weeks he was supposed to go back into that jungle.

SIX

"It's bedtime, Lisa," Stephie insisted, but with an indulgent glint in her eyes. Lisa practiced the usual set of delays and they'd gone through them all.

"One more story," Lisa pleaded, but her eyes said she understood that wouldn't be forthcoming.

"No more stories." Stephie was firm. "But I'll leave the night light on for you."

"I love you, Mommie." Lisa reached up for a final hug.

Stephie headed out for the kitchen to do the dishes. She glanced out the window at the night sky, devoid of stars or moon. The weather people predicted a thunderstorm tonight. She'd have to do something soon about repairing the roof. Tom never got around to fixing it and two years later she was still struggling with money, dreading the possible need of a new roof.

The phone was a noisy intrusion in the silence of the house. She hurried out to the living room to respond.

"Hello?"

"Hi." Gary's voice came to her. "I missed

seeing you when I went in for breakfast this morning." Gary had rarely missed a morning for breakfast in the past eight months. The whole crew knew he was there to see her. "I knew it was your day off, of course, and you'll be off tomorrow again." An edge of desperation in his voice.

"Gary, you know what Mr Allen said. I'm not to go out with anybody until the divorce papers are finally signed."

"Yeah, I know . . ." He sighed. "And you said starting this week the restaurant will be closed for dinners." She was sure it was hard on his budget, but in the busy months when she worked the dinner shift as well as breakfast and lunch, he'd contrived to come for dinner once or twice a week.

"Just till after New Year's," she reminded. Gary was so sweet. She wasn't in love with him, but that might come some day.

"When are your parents heading for Florida?"

"They're flying out tomorrow morning." They'd be back two days before Christmas, always a big family event. Two tables pulled together to accommodate the mob: her married brothers, their wives, their children, plus the aunts and uncles who made the annual trek for Christmas in Montauk.

"Can I talk to Lisa?" A tenderness in his voice now. He was truly fond of her.

"Lisa's asleep —" she began.

"No I'm not!" Lisa called back. "If that's

Gary, I want to tell him good-night."

"All right," Stephie agreed. "Hold on, Gary —"

She was conscious of the threat of tears while she listened to the spirited conversation between Lisa and Gary. He was so sweet to her. To Tom Lisa was just somebody to use to get back at *her*. He'd never been a real father. There'd been moments, yes, when he was proud of his adorable small daughter. But he'd never changed a diaper, never walked the floor with her when she was teething, was never there to comfort her when she was sick. She was a toy who occasionally amused him.

"All right, Lisa, enough," she broke in. "Back to bed." She reached for the phone. "I have to tuck her in again. See you Wednesday at breakfast."

"Mommie —" Lisa paused, her smile wistful. "Will Gary be my new daddy some day?"

Stephie was startled. "We'll see," she hedged.

Lisa wanted a full-time daddy like her three friends in her day care group. There was no way she could have stayed with Tom. That was a bad deal for both her and Lisa. Gary would be a wonderful father — that was a major point in his favor.

Paul Hamilton must be a great father to his two sons. I've never known anybody quite like him.

Where was Diane these days? Was she married? Did she have children? Had she become an actress, the way she dreamed? How long since

50

she'd heard from Diane? Five, no, almost six years. Diane's parents had bought their 'second home' in Montauk when she and Diane were twelve. She'd waited impatiently through the long, cold, blustery winters for Diane and her family to start their weekend treks, that became full-time occupancy once Diane and her brother were out of school for the year.

Every St Patrick's Day weekend Diane and her family came out for the parade that said, 'The season's opening soon!' She and Diane would stand along the route and watch the fire trucks that came from all over the Island, cheer on the Montauk Library float that was special to both of them. During the school year she and Diane exchanged letters regularly, always writing about what each was reading. Then there was the long drought between St Patrick's Day and Memorial Day, when Diane and her family began to come out for weekends.

She'd hoped up to the day that she graduated high school that Mom and Dad would agree to her going away to college. At hopeful moments she'd thought that Grandma would help her. Even eight years ago it cost a lot of money to go away to college. For a while she'd thought about applying to Southampton College, where she could commute. But Mom and Dad had made it clear. Her brother Joe was getting married and moving down the Island, where his future father-in-law ran a restaurant. The family needed her to come into the business.

She closed her eyes, remembering that last Memorial Day weekend when Diane had been here. They were both graduating high school in June. Diane was going to Vassar in the fall. Stephie would be working at the restaurant . . .

"I think it's terrible that you're not going to college," Diane said indignantly. "You graduated first in your class — your grades were terrific."

"Maybe if I was a boy . . ." Stephie shrugged. "But none of my brothers was much of a student. They just managed to get through high school." In truth, Vinnie dropped out in his senior year, using the business as his excuse.

"Your parents are so old-fashioned." Diane grunted in disgust. "They're living in the last century."

"When will you start college?" *It's not fair that I can't go too.*

"Early." Diane sounded both excited and fearful, Stephie thought. "Mom says we'll have to go back into the city by the middle of August so we can shop for my clothes." She hesitated. "But I'll be out here as soon as school closes." Diane went to private school so that meant she'd be here the first week in June.

"Will you come out here next summer?" Already she felt a sense of loss.

"Oh, sure. You know I love Montauk."

But Diane hadn't come out the following summer. She'd gone to Europe with a group from her college. All through her freshman year she'd written at intervals. She'd sent a postcard from Paris that summer. After that they'd sort of lost touch with each other.

If she could have gone to college, she'd never have married Tom. She and Diane used to talk about the kind of men they expected to marry. Oh, God, their crazy dreams. She was going to be a teacher and Diane was going to be an actress. *'Not a movie star, a stage actress.'* Each summer she and Diane devoured plays they found in the library: Shaw, Ibsen, Eugene O'Neill.

But once out of school she was lonely — and rebellious. At home she was still treated like a child. The others in her graduating class, except for the ones who went off to college, married early. It was an escape from home, a need to feel independent.

Tom had been so sweet when they were going out together. She wasn't in love with him but he made her feel special. She hadn't realised he figured he was marrying into money. She was the only girl in the family and he thought Mom and Dad would buy them a house, maybe put him into some kind of business. He couldn't even hold down a steady job!

Paul switched off the TV set after watching *The NewsHour with Jim Lehrer*. It was eight o'clock. Time to go out for dinner. What places were open this time of year? He reached for the copy of *The Pioneer* which he'd picked up at the IGA, flipped through the pages. He heard the first rumble of thunder that blended with the sound of the rough surf pounding the shore. He would have dinner here. He wasn't a gourmet chef, but he could always handle a pasta dinner.

He went into the kitchen and hunted in the cabinets until he located the proper utensil. He filled the pot with water, smiling in recall of pasta dinners he'd made occasionally for himself and the kids when Emily was working late and Melinda off for the night. Mark and Larry were great kids. Melinda, mature and loving, was a treasure of a nanny, after three bad tries.

He brought out pasta and a bottle of sauce, paused in inner debate. Sure, call home. The boys would be giving Melinda their usual pitch about 'I'm thirsty' or 'I have to go to the bathroom.' The usual night-time ritual. They'd still be awake.

He reached for the kitchen phone to call home. God, how had people survived before Bell invented the phone? He heard the ring at the other end, waited.

"Hello, the Hamilton residence." Melinda's crisp British accent had won her approval from Ted Gorman. *'These British nannies know how to handle kids. None of the crazy spoiling American parents indulge in these days.'*

"Melinda, is Emily home yet?" No formality in this family, he prided himself.

"No, she called and said the boys were not to

wait up for her. I gather you'll want to say good-night to them."

"Yes, please."

As usual when he phoned and talked with them, Mark and Larry entered into good-humored squabbling about who was to talk first. First Mark, then Larry reported on the day's activities. Then Mark insisted on a final few words.

"Daddy, when are you coming home?" His voice was simultaneously plaintive and querulous.

"Hey, Mark, this is my first night away," Paul scolded.

"But you were in the hospital, and now you're away again."

"I'll be home soon," he promised. Three weeks to a six-year-old would sound like a life-time. "Here's a big hug and a kiss — and go to sleep. Tell Mommie I called. Tomorrow," he added, lest Mark try to use this as an excuse to postpone bedtime.

He stood motionless beside the phone for a few minutes. Would he ever get over this guilt about being away from the kids so much? Emily clung to the conviction that the 'quality time' they provided compensated for the time they were away. A phrase created to console working mothers. Yet she'd talked with such pain about being shunted off to nannies, then boarding schools when she was a child.

Emily worked hard at being a mother, he told

himself defensively. No matter how late she worked — and work often included late night socializing — she was up before seven o'clock to get the kids up and give them breakfast, rather than leaving this to Melinda. And he was up with her for this morning ritual. And on weekends, except those where business intruded, he and Emily devoted every waking hour to Mark and Larry.

They were good parents. Weren't they?

Stephie's alarm went off. Without opening her eyes she reached to shut it off, secure in the knowledge that in five minutes it would ring again. What crazy dreams she'd had last night! She froze in self-conscious recall. She'd dreamt about Paul Hamilton, and how both of them were teaching in some inner city high school. But your dreams evolved from what you'd talked about during the previous day. It wasn't so strange that she'd dreamt about him.

Tuesday, her mind registered. Her second day off. She should take advantage of it. Starting January she'd be working two jobs. She lay back against the pillows, eyes wide now, contemplating the day ahead. Early morning sunlight filtered in through the drapes. It was going to be a beautiful day.

She lingered in bed waiting for the second warning from the alarm clock. Had Mr Allen talked to Tom's attorney yet? Tom didn't expect to get away with this joint custody deal, did he?

Why did he want it? But she knew the answer: to torment her. The alarm clock emitted its second and final warning.

She threw aside the blankets and hurried out to raise the thermostat. For an hour the house would be blissfully warm. She'd drop it again when they left. The *Farmers Almanac*, Grandma said, predicted a mild winter. Let it be — in deference to her oil bills.

In a flannel robe and fleece-lined slippers, she went into the laundry room, separated from the bathroom by only a louvered door, to do a load of laundry while the house was heating up. By then the bathroom would be warm enough to shower. She wouldn't use the dryer today, instead hang things up to dry without running up the electric bill. Her LILCO bills could be horrendous.

Closing the bathroom door to soften the rumble of the washing machine, she went to Lisa's tiny but charming bedroom.

"The sun's shining," Lisa said triumphantly. She was awake. She always waited for this small morning ritual when mother and daughter discussed the day's plans.

"Lisa, how would you like to spend the morning with me?" She felt a rush of warmth as Lisa's eyes lighted. "I'm not working today. We could go for a long walk on the beach, and then you could go supermarket shopping with me. We'll go over to Grandma's for lunch, then you can play with your friends at Dorothy's house in

the afternoon." She'd make Dorothy understand she was paying the usual weekly fee. She
wasn't trying to cut back on her money.

"Can we have pizza for lunch?" Lisa's face was
aglow with anticipation.

"It's not polite to tell Grandma what to serve.
But I'll bet she'll have pizza in the freezer." She
and Grandma might show their enormous love,
but Lisa was not spoiled.

She thought about children who came into the
restaurant with parents who had little time to
give them, who considered spoiling the way to
make up for this.

'Jonnie, where do you want to sit?' a mother
would ask a rebellious three-year-old.

They permitted their small children to roam
about the restaurant, disturbing other diners
because it was easier not to discipline, Stephie
thought in distaste. That wasn't doing a child a
favor. Discipline belonged in everybody's survival kit.

Over breakfast she and Lisa talked about
Chloe. Thank God, she'd gotten Lisa out of her
determination to eat macaroni and cheese three
times a day. It was all right to have it once or
twice a week for lunch at Dorothy's house, she'd
finally convinced Lisa, but it was important to
eat other things, like vegetables and fruit. Now,
telling Lisa how she'd run into Chloe on the
beach yesterday, she asked herself yet again if
Lisa had forgotten that Saturday with her father.
She'd been subdued — upset without knowing

58

why — for several days. Lisa was so young, Grandma insisted, she'd put that ugly scene out of her mind.

"Can we feed the gulls?" Lisa interrupted her introspection. "Can we?"

"Sure," Stephie agreed. "We'll take along some bread."

In a corner of her mind she thought about Paul Hamilton. Would he be on the beach this morning, too?

SEVEN

Paul relished the morning quiet. The aroma of fresh coffee filtering through the house translated into a sense of well-being. The sunlight poured through the sliders. For the first time, he thought, he truly understood the concept of solar heating. Standing before a slider and gazing out onto the unexpectedly calm ocean, he felt enveloped in the warmth of the sun.

The phone rang. He went to pick it up. Again, it was a wrong number. Last night he'd half-expected Emily to call when she came home, even if it was late. She knew he'd become an insomniac these last months. He'd thought the wrong number would be a call from her. But she was respecting his need to get away, he scolded himself. Why the hell was she so pissed that he chose to come here instead of flying down to the Caribbean? It wasn't as though she could have gone down there with him.

Enjoy these weeks, he exhorted himself. Live each day at a time. The faint swoosh from the coffee-maker told him the coffee was ready. He went into the kitchen, poured the strong, black liquid into a mug. He'd eat later, just have his coffee and go for a long walk on the beach. There wouldn't be a more perfect day than this one. Not a cloud in the sky, the wind a soft whisper, the water a radiant blue. Instinct told him this wouldn't be an ever-changing day like yesterday.

He drank in appreciative gulps, grimacing as he recalled the swill he consumed at irregular intervals during each working day. Never time, it seemed, to go out for a decent lunch. His group at the office was shockingly small compared to other departments, but it was a powerhouse, where much of the profits were made.

Ted Gorman moved in an elite circle high above his own, but his father-in-law had placed him where he could move into unbelievable money in a short time. Derivatives salesmen earned the most money, walked off with the largest bonuses other than those accorded the top officers. Why had making huge sums of money seemed so irresistible that first year?

Ted's bonus last year was three million dollars — before taxes, as he made a point of reminding. And he had substantial alimony payments to two ex-wives. But he was doing well by his only grandsons, Paul conceded. Pushing sixty, he'd developed grandfatherly sentiments, the kind that had eluded him as a father. Emily's mother had seen Mark three times since he was born, Larry once.

He rinsed the mug, debated for a moment about cleaning out the fireplace before hitting the beach. No, let it wait for later. He was conscious of an urgency to be striding over the pristine beach, breathing in the soft damp air. He hurried down the stairs to the beach with a sense of exhilaration.

Will Stephie be on the beach this morning? Why am I so drawn to her? This is crazy. I love Emily, we have a good marriage. All right, it was good until we got ourselves on this money merry-go-round. Other couples have kids and they don't suddenly go berserk on a money chase. Why don't I just say to Emily, 'I can't be a derivatives salesman — I need to teach.' We don't have to have a big, fancy apartment and a car to match. Other couples with two kids live on less money. Why can't we?

All at once he realised he was perspiring despite the cold. Don't think about what waited for him back in New York, he told himself. The gigantic mortgage payments on the condo, the car loan, the car insurance, the monthly garage bill, Melinda's salary, the fancy tuition bills for Mark and Larry. Put that out of his mind for now. Use these three weeks to heal.

But will it be any easier when I go back? No. We're out of step with reality, but how do we find our way back?

He paused at the water's edge, debated about which direction to take. Towards the Point or the other way? Then in the distance he spied a small figure in a red jacket. Stephie, he decided with a flurry of anticipation. This time he was sure. A tiny figure beside her. That would be her daughter. Lisa, he recalled.

They were standing before a cluster of sea-gulls, he realised as he approached them. Lisa was a minute replica of her mother, he thought with sudden tenderness. She was tossing bread crumbs to the gulls, ecstatically engrossed in this activity. What a beautiful portrait they made, mother, daughter, seagulls, with the ocean and sky as a backdrop.

"Hi!" An element of surprise blended with pleasure in her greeting. "It's going to be a glorious day —"

"At this time of the year days like this are a precious gift."

"This is Lisa," Stephie said. "Of course, she's too busy at the moment to acknowledge an introduction —" She frowned. "Do you suppose bread is good for the gulls?"

"It's a treat for them from the way they're going for it." He laughed as Lisa tossed a crumb and a gull flew up to catch it mid-air. "It's not something they get every day."

"The day's so beautiful I decided to keep Lisa with me until after lunch, then she can go to her play group." Her eyes rested lovingly on her daughter. "Play group sounds nicer than sitter, don't you think?"

"Definitely." She was in a light mood today, he thought in approval, but a moment later her eyes seemed to lose their glow.

"Don't you like the sitter?" He and Emily were lucky to have Melinda.

"Oh, she's great." Stephie seemed startled by the question. "It's just that sometimes I feel guilty that I'm away from her so much. I suppose most working mothers feel that way —"

"Emily — my wife," he explained, "keeps telling me it's quality time that counts. But she worries, too." *If I were a teacher, I could spend more time with the kids. Wouldn't that lessen some of Emily's stress, knowing I was with them?*

"I didn't work until Lisa was seven months old — then it wasn't a matter of choice anymore." She spread her hands in an eloquent gesture. "My grandmother's been wonderful, but she bakes and does some of the cooking for the restaurant — she can't put that aside to take care of Lisa full time.

"In another year or so Lisa will be in kindergarten, and then it'll be first grade and school till three o'clock.

"If I had a job like teaching, I'd be able to do without child care once she's in first grade. I could pick her up after school and we'd go home together." Wistfulness was replaced by frustration. "But during the season I'm working crazy hours, and off-season I'm doing two jobs to survive." She managed a wisp of laughter. "I sound like somebody in a soap opera!"

"I'm sure it's not easy being a single mother." Was it any easier, he asked himself, to be a single father? Nobody talked about that. But then few men found themselves in that position.

"I suspect that for most people life is a fight for

survival." But her eyes said she doubted that this applied to him. Damn. He'd told her yesterday about being in investment banking and how the money even at this stage was four times what he'd earn teaching. Did she think he was lucky to be making so much money?

"Oooh! Don't go away!" Lisa wailed because the gulls were taking off in nervous haste as Chloe sauntered towards them. "Come back!"

"Lisa, they're afraid of Chloe," Stephie soothed and reached to pat Chloe's silken head. "Say 'Hello,' Lisa."

"I love you, Chloe." Lisa flung both arms about the affectionate Bernese. "Good doggie."

"Mark and Larry love dogs, too," Paul felt a sudden yearning to reach out and embrace his sons, "but with our crazy hours we didn't dare take on that responsibility. I mean, in the city you can't just open the door and let them go out for a run."

Suddenly, with an intensity that unnerved him, their eyes met and clung. The air heavy with unspoken emotions. *What's happening to us?* He knew that she, too, shared these tumultuous feelings that almost suffocated him.

"Lisa, we have to go." Stephie's voice was taut, almost frightened. "I have a million errands to do this morning," she told Paul. "I hope you enjoy your walk." She reached a hand out to Lisa. "Lisa, we have to go now —"

"What are we going to do, Mommie?" A faint

65

reproach in Lisa's voice as she sat beside her mother in the car.

Stephie understood; Lisa had wanted to stay on the beach. How could she tell her precious baby that she'd stood there beside Paul Hamilton and felt suddenly terrified. It was as though another person was taking over her mind, her emotions. She'd felt almost out of control, as though strange forces were about to re-direct her life.

"Mommie . . ." Lisa prodded.

"We have to go to Becker's to buy a new skillet." She forced herself back to the moment. "Then to Claudia's to buy a birthday present for Grandma." Lisa adored wandering about Claudia's Carriage House — admiring the wonderful stuffed animals, the elegant dolls, the array of jewelry and choice gift items.

"When's her birthday?" Lisa's face brightened. She was envisioning a luscious birthday cake, Stephie interpreted.

"Not for a month," Stephie conceded, "but I thought we ought to have it ready. But you mustn't tell Grandma what it is." To Lisa her great-grandmother was Grandma. Her grandmother was Nana.

"What will we choose?" Lisa was avidly involved in this improvised project.

"Oh, we'll look around and see all the wonderful goodies Claudia buys for the shop and then we'll decide." *What's happening to me that I can feel this way about Paul Hamilton? What makes*

66

him so special that I want to feel his arms about me? That I want him to hold me so close I can barely breathe? I've never felt this way about anybody.

They drove to Main Street, went into Becker's. With the skillet bought they headed across to Claudia's Carriage House, where Lisa lingered in admiration before every exquisite doll, every appealing stuffed animal. With Lisa brought into the final choosing, they settled on a jewelry chest that was a miniature replica of an eighteenth-century American highboy as Grandma's birthday gift.

"We'll go to Grandma's now," Stephie decided. "But we don't tell her about the present. Cross your heart." And Lisa solemnly obeyed.

Stephie always felt a kind of peace in the Bertonelli kitchen. This was Grandma's domain. Aromas of cakes and cookies baking in the oven, tantalizing sauces simmering on the impressive range, were a statement to her that all was right in the world. Here with Grandma she could, for a parcel of time, forget her personal woes.

"Lisa, if I give you some dough, will you make me some of those tiny twisted rolls I like?" Grandma cajoled, and Lisa nodded vigorously.

But today the kitchen's magic was eroding. Had Mr Allen called the house? While the other two involved themselves in rolling out dough, Stephie reached to the kitchen phone to call home. No messages on the machine. She hesitated, then dialed Mr Allen's office, asked to speak with him.

"Just one minute, Stephie," his secretary said, her voice sympathetic.

She frowned, waiting for the lawyer to come to the phone.

"Stephie, I have nothing to report. But . . ." he hesitated, "I have a feeling his attorney is waiting for Tom to come across with some back payments before he pursues this —"

"But what are we supposed to do?" A stridency in her voice now.

"Cool it, Stephie. I'll give him a few days, then threaten to withdraw the cash offer. That'll bring us some action."

"I'm just so tired of this." And tired of being billed for every small conversation. Was Grandma right in thinking that maybe she ought to look for another lawyer?

"As soon as I have anything to report, I'll call you," he promised. "I have to leave for court now."

EIGHT

Paul thrust aside the paperback he'd been trying to read. He was still too tense to focus on a novel. He left the comfortable lounge chair, crossed to add another log to the fire in the grate. Frowning, he fiddled with the dial of the radio. What was the number of the NPR station in the area? Ah, this must be it, he thought in satisfaction as the strains of a Beethoven sonata filled the room. Thank God for National Public Radio.

He was conscious now of hunger, strolled out to the kitchen to consider what to prepare for lunch. He opened the refrigerator to stare at the contents. A turkey sandwich, warmed in the toaster oven, and a tall mug of tea, he decided. He slid slabs of turkey breast between slices of bread, then as an afterthought added mustard. The sandwich in the toaster oven, he poured water into the tea kettle, feeling oddly relaxed at performing these small tasks.

With his lunch on a tray he headed out to the deck, warmed by the sun despite normal December temperature. He ate with gusto for the first time in many weeks, glorying in his escape from the trading floor. His gaze swept the expanse of beach before him. A few gulls hovered at the water's edge. A lone male jogged, a dog at his heels. Why had Stephie dashed off so suddenly this morning?

He finished his meal, deposited mug and plate on the deck beside the chaise. He closed his eyes, willed himself to sleep. Much later he was awakened by the harsh ring of the phone. Hell, why hadn't he brought the cordless out here with him?

He hurried inside, picked up the receiver. "Hello?"

"Mr Hamilton?" a male voice asked.

"That's right." Somebody trying to sell him something out here?

"This is Bill Ryan. I'm the house-watcher for the property. Mrs Hamilton phoned to ask me to order half a cord of logs. I just wanted to let you know it'll be delivered first thing tomorrow morning."

"Thank you. I'll be glad to have them." In her crazy schedule Emily had found time to make sure he had a supply of logs. She knew how much he enjoyed a wood-burning fireplace.

He and Emily had found each other early in their junior year of college. She'd had such a zest for living, he remembered. The two of them and Bobbie and Steve Michaels had spent much of their free time together their junior and senior years at Columbia. Subconsciously he smiled, visualizing evenings in Emily's condo on Riverside Drive.

Bobbie and Steve had married during the spring break of their senior year. They were both going on to mod school. He closed his eyes and recalled the night before graduation. They'd shopped at Zabar's for dinner makings, sat for hours talking about their futures . . .

"Okay, so you guys have it over me," Emily had conceded in high spirits. "I'm not sure what I want to do, though this public relations job my dad wangled for me sounds like fun."

"Bobbie and I have got a long row ahead of us." Steve was unfamiliarly somber. "The years at med school, more years as residents. But it's what we both want."

"I'm not sure I could survive it alone," Bobbie admitted, "but with Steve I can hack it."

"We'll get the hell out of this town," Steve said, shuddering. "I want to practice in some small town where our patients won't just be numbers on a chart. Where living costs are low, and we can keep our fees small enough so patients won't be afraid to come to us."

"I just want to teach." Paul radiated dedication. "Like my parents. I'll never make a lot of money but it'll be a satisfying life."

"We won't need a lot of money," Emily said softly. "We'll have each other. That's the important thing."

Three days later he and Emily were married at City Hall. They hadn't wanted a big wedding but he knew that Emily was disappointed that there was no religious ceremony. Later, they promised themselves, hating the coldness of the City Hall ceremony.

Emily's mother was off somewhere in Europe — Emily hadn't heard from her in many months. Her father had several business trips scheduled, couldn't seem to settle on a free day. So Bobbie and Steve had gone with them to City Hall.

Three weeks after their City Hall ceremony, when they were moving into their first apartment, Emily's father took them out for a sumptuous dinner and told them his wedding gift would be an Acura Legend. During the next year Emily invited him to dinner at their apartment near Gramercy Park for holiday dinners — Thanksgiving, Christmas, Easter. And from the moment Emily told him she was pregnant, he'd been determined to run their lives.

Not until Emily's father presented them with the Acura Legend as though with some casual trinket, did Paul realize that her family was super-rich. That dropped a net of guilt over him. He was taking her into another, less comfortable, world. He'd known vaguely that the borrowed studio condo she'd lived in the last two years at Columbia belonged to an aunt, who kept it as a *Pied-à-terre* — unused for the past three years. Not until he was part of the firm did he understand the kind of bonuses his father-in-law received each year, atop a huge salary.

Clint said that before the 1990s the firm had a reputation for high ethics. He'd called it a top tier 'white-shoe' company . . .

"Then came the big drive on derivatives, and the whole scene changed," Clint drawled. "Sure, some investors got tired of being screwed and cut out in the last year or so, but derivatives are still what earns the firm astronomical profits."

"You make it sound like a game." An ugly, vicious game.

"I think even if I was loaded to the gills, with more money than I could ever spend, I'd stay with the business. For me it's the biggest, most exciting, game in town."

"Doesn't it bother you when pension funds, insurance funds are gambled on derivatives? Can you imagine what those losses mean to millions of people?"

"That's their problem, not mine." Clint chuckled. "I've told you a dozen times. In this business you need the killer instinct, and I've got it."

Emily got upset when he tried to talk to her about what happened on the trading floor. How people, because they just didn't understand that they were taking such risks, were suffering terrible losses. And the firm took advantage of those times to push them into taking even further losses. She hadn't known what happened at Gorman, Tremont & Ashford. And now she tried to block it out of her mind.

I should have been firm, refused to go back for an MBA, refused to go to work for the firm. But all of a sudden, with Mark on the way, the future seemed ominous. But don't think about that now. Try to unwind. That's why I'm out here. To clear my head, learn how to cope with tomorrow. I'll go to the local library tomorrow, pick out some of the classics I've never found time to read. Thoreau's Walden, *for starters.*

He'd ask around town about the availability of a library. Stephie would know that — she was the kind who would have made the library her home away from home when she was growing up, the way he had. Would he run into her again? Sure, he decided with self-conscious anticipation — she loved the beach the way he did.

Restless, he decided to walk on the beach again. Amazed that this treasure still belonged to him alone, except for a teenage pair who walked arm-in-arm and stopped at intervals to wrap themselves into a passionate embrace. Oblivious to his presence as he strode past them.

Stephie was in the midst of an ugly divorce, he recalled with compassion. Like Emily and himself she'd married young. She couldn't be more than twenty-five or twenty-six. Sad to be breaking up when there was a small child involved. Seeing her with her little girl, Lisa, he knew she was a loving, dedicated mother.

Back from his walk, he fell asleep on the sofa before the fireplace, where logs still smoldered. He awoke to find night descending, left the sofa to gaze out at the darkening sky. Damn, he'd missed the sunset. It must have been magnificent after a day like this. But he'd napped again and that was good, part of his recovery.

He debated about dinner. Too lazy to go out, he decided to settle for what was in the refrigerator. Throw a chicken cutlet on the electric grill, stir-fry a mess of vegetables. Finish off with frozen yogurt and coffee.

After dinner he abandoned his 'no TV' regime, checked in on *The NewsHour with Jim Lehrer*, switched from TV to radio after that. His second night away from the apartment. He'd never been apart from Mark and Larry this long. They'd be in bed by now. Don't call and wake them. Yet he felt a nagging need to hear their voices. To talk with Emily.

In the years when he was teaching, he'd come home from school — except on those afternoons when he was busy with after-school activities — and start dinner preparations. Sure, most times it was dinner courtesy of Citarella's or Zabar's take-out, but they sat down together, happy to be with each other. He talked about his students. She talked about her clients. They'd both loved what they were doing.

He glanced at his watch. Mark and Larry were asleep by now but Emily might be home. Suddenly it was urgent to touch base. He reached for the cordless phone, settled himself before the fire, and tapped out the apartment number, willing Emily to be home.

"Hello?" Emily's voice.

"Hi. You sound tired," he commiserated.

"Oh, it's been a bitch of a day. I just walked in five minutes ago."

"The boys asleep?"

"Yeah, they were off before I got in." A defensive tone in her voice. "Melinda says they're fine."

"It was a gorgeous day out here. I was pissed that I fell asleep and missed the sunset."

"You'd have had gorgeous sunsets at St John's or St Bart's."

"What's this fixation you have about my going down there instead of coming out here?" He tried to sound amused.

"I feel like such an idiot telling people you're recovering from pneumonia at Montauk."

"You're in a rotten mood," he joshed.

"Sometimes I wonder what I'm doing in this insane business." An unfamiliar bitterness in her voice startled him. "I had lunch with three different people today. I feel like I have a stopwatch in my head."

"How could you eat three lunches? Where would you put it?" She was pencil-slim.

"Oh, you know the new craziness in this town." She sighed. "Nobody has enough time to do business, we all need another five hours each day. I had lunch with a new client at twelve-fifteen. Thirty minutes later he excuses himself — 'Sorry, darling, but you know how it is. So much to do in the course of one day' — and he pops off to another table — which I'm not supposed to notice — and I dash three blocks away to have lunch with an old client who's griping we're not getting him enough TV coverage. He comes right out and admits he only has time for a 'quickie'. And I'm off to a third lunch, where they promise a gourmet meal in thirty minutes."

"It sounds maddening," he sympathized. He'd heard much, of course, about the new business lunches where nobody drank and the menu was light. Long gone were the three-martini, two-hour luncheons.

"Aren't you getting bored out there?" Emily asked.

"Not yet. I'm doing a lot of sleeping." *I've only been here about forty-eight hours.*

"Paul, I'm starving," she apologized. "Let me see what I can find for a quick dinner. And keep sleeping a lot. That's good for you."

Off the phone, he sat immobile, staring into the grey-edged ruddy embers in the fireplace without seeing. Emily never admitted to being annoyed with her job. At intervals she bitched about a difficult client but she'd never said she disliked her work. Most of the time she was upbeat about it.

Did she figure on working until he came up with a real killing, then cutting out of that scene? She never said a word about it. Was she waiting for them to be financially secure so she could quit the business? Her querulous complaint tickertaped across his mind now: *'Sometimes I wonder what I'm doing in this insane business.'* He felt a knot tightening in his stomach, a pounding in his head.

Emily's counting on me to be a successful deriva-tives salesman so she can afford to quit her job. God, how can I go back to that jungle?

NINE

Stephie had been conscious of a slight drizzle during the night. She awoke to a dank, cold, fog-drenched morning. No prospect of watching the sun rise this morning. She hurried from her bed to the thermostat in the hallway, shivering in the cold air. In fifteen minutes the house would be comfortable. Then she'd wake Lisa. Though she dreaded driving in a heavy fog, she felt a kind of serenity on mornings like this. Fog brought a sense of being cosseted, of being protected from harsh realities.

Would this cause a delay in Mom and Dad's departure this morning? Thank God, Vinnie would be driving them down to MacArthur to make their flight. She wouldn't have to make that morning crawl through the fog all the way down there. She'd be a nervous wreck.

Wrapped now in a plaid flannel robe, feet in the thermal booties Gary had given her for her birthday last month, she went out to the kitchen to put up coffee. She'd give Lisa breakfast, have her own at the restaurant. She inspected the kitchen ceiling. No sign of a leak, but there'd been no more than a drizzle last night.

By six-forty she'd showered, dressed, awakened and prepared Lisa for the day, and served her breakfast. Paul might be walking on the beach, she thought involuntarily, the way she did sometimes. It was eerie yet exhilarating to walk on the beach when visibility was no more than thirty or forty feet, the ocean obscured by the fog. But no beach walk this morning, she rejected. No time for that.

Will Paul be on the beach? Why is my heart pounding this way? He's a stranger, we barely know each other.

"Lisa, it's late." Her voice was sharper than she intended as she forced herself back to reality. "Let's get you into your jacket."

"Can I take my new box of magic markers with me?" Lisa extended an arm into the jacket sleeve. "I told Dorothy I would."

"Sure you can. Where did you leave them?"

"I'll get them." Lisa darted towards the living room coffee table to retrieve the box.

Thank God, Lisa was long past the period when she'd cried each morning as they approached Dorothy's house. Though Dorothy said the minute Stephie was out the door and headed for the car, Lisa had stopped crying.

The phone rang. Frowning, Stephie picked up the receiver.

"Hello."

"Honey, I just wanted to tell you I'll be working all week over near Riverhead. I won't be able to come in for breakfast." Gary was plainly disappointed.

"That happens every now and then," she sympathised. "But your boss keeps you working," she added with approval. Tom never held on to a job for more than a few weeks.

"I shouldn't be talking about it yet," a hint of excitement in his voice, "but there's a chance my boss might take me in the business — you know, as a partner. He knows I'm a hard worker, I'm conscientious. He knows he can depend on me."

"Gary, that's wonderful!"

"I better run. It's a long haul to Riverhead."

Stephie drove the two miles to Dorothy's house with the care the foggy conditions demanded. As usual, she was the first of the parents to arrive. She exchanged a few words with Dorothy, then headed back to the car. She'd be arriving late. Vinnie couldn't leave until she was there. She hovered over the wheel, her eyes fastened to the lights of the car just ahead. In weather like this it was a routine of following the leader.

The restaurant windows were steamed over. She welcomed the rush of heat as she opened the door and walked inside. The first of the morning patrons straddled seats at the counter, the tables still unoccupied. Mom and Dad waited, luggage at their feet.

"I got here as fast as I could," she apologised, though a glance at the clock told her they'd still arrive in time for their flight — probably delayed due to the fog.

"You know your mom," Dad grumbled. "She

pushed all the clocks ahead twenty minutes, as usual when we have to be somewhere."

"That's why we get places on time," Mom shot back. "Vinnie!" she called. "Let's go."

Vinnie, stocky, quick to anger, a replica of his father, ambled into view. "Ma, we'll make the plane. Stop worryin'."

Stephie took her place behind the counter, exchanged the customary banter with the pair of would-be stand-up comics devouring their usual eggs, sausages and toast. Minutes after Vinnie pulled away from the curb, the phone rang. Stephie hurried to answer.

"Good-morning, The Oasis."

"Stephie, has Vinnie left yet?" Sara, his long-time girlfriend, asked anxiously.

"Just this minute. He's taking Mom and Dad down to the airport."

"Yeah, I figured." Sara sighed. "I wanted to ask him about coming to dinner an hour earlier tonight. There's this slide show at the library that I'm dying to see."

"I'll tell him," Stephie promised. "We won't be open for dinner so he should be able to make it."

They talked a few moments more, then Stephie excused herself. The morning breakfast crowd was coming through the door. There'd be a steady rush for the next hour and a half, then business would slow down to a trickle until lunchtime. That was the winter scene.

Not until close to nine o'clock did the phone

ring again. This time the caller was Grandma.

"Did they get off in time?"

"On the button," Stephie said. "They should make it even with the foggy road conditions this morning."

"I don't like them flying in this weather."

"Grandma, they'll be fine." Stephie's voice was tender. "You'll be at church praying for them."

"God expects us to use our heads. Why couldn't they cancel and go tomorrow? I know," she added before Stephie could reply, "your father couldn't wait another day to get down there. So," she said after a moment, "did Mom talk to Vinnie about Sara?" Grandma had been on Mom's back to push Vinnie into proposing.

"I don't know . . ." Vinnie and Sara had been going together for eleven years, since he was nineteen and she seventeen.

"I told Sara what was wrong." Grandma was not loathe to speak her mind in what she considered a good cause. "Why should Vinnie marry her, take on the responsibilities of a husband, when he's getting it for free?"

"But she's not listening," Stephie said gently. Sara was scared to death of losing Vinnie, who was strong on macho good looks but weak in the brain department.

"Call the airport and see if the plane's leaving on time. Let me know, Stephie."

"Sure, Grandma."

Why did Sara put up with Vinnie, Stephie

asked herself in annoyance. Let a few years go by and he'd dump her for some teenage slut. Sara had been going with Vinnie when *she* was fifteen. She'd married, had a child, and was getting a divorce — and Sara was still waiting for Vinnie to propose.

Please God, let the divorce come through. Should I call Mr Allen again? No, Grandma's right. Wait for him to call me. But when will that be?

Paul lingered over breakfast at Mr John's Pancake House. He was amazed that he'd slept so late this morning. But then sleep had been slow in overtaking him. He couldn't erase from his mind that unexpected bitterness he'd heard in Emily's voice when she talked about her job. He'd thought — she'd given him every indication — that she felt about her career the way he felt about teaching. When did that terrific enthusiasm ebb away? Now it was the money that was the big attraction but the game had lost its savor. And the pressure was on him.

Despite the fog, in truth, enjoying it, he'd walked for almost an hour before coming in for breakfast, surprised to feel such hunger this morning. Emily complained he looked gaunt. If he continued to pack away food the way he did this morning, that complaint would disappear.

Though he'd known it was unlikely, he'd nurtured a hope that he'd see Stephie on the beach this morning. Compulsively his eyes had focused on the fog ahead, willing her to emerge into

84

view. It was irrational to feel this need to see someone he'd met in a casual encounter.

He smiled, nodded at the waitress who approached with coffee refills. No rush, he had no appointments to keep.

I don't have to plan my day; it's open for whatever arrives. Go over to Martell's, pick up the New York Times. *Go home and read it cover to cover. When have I had time for that since going into the jungle?*

Zipping up his jacket against the damp cold, he left the Pancake House and strode up Main Street to Martell's to pick up his newspaper, conscious of the closed-up shops on either side of the street. At Martell's he enquired about the local library, asked for directions. Okay, this afternoon he'd go over to the library and pick up the Thoreau. Stretch out before the fireplace and read. Forget about everything else.

At the house he piled a pyramid of logs in the fireplace grate, spent a few moments coaxing a healthy blaze into being, then settled himself on the sofa to read the *Times.* Before he'd reached the OP-ED page he'd drifted off to sleep again. The sea air and his hearty breakfast, he thought when he came slowly awake again.

What was the name of the restaurant where Stephie worked? The family restaurant, he recalled. He could drive down there for lunch, on a casual sightseeing expedition. No, his mind rejected. Don't be so pushy. Besides, he hadn't the faintest idea of the name of the place.

Maybe he'd run into her on the beach

tomorrow. She said she liked to walk early in the morning. Didn't she? He felt a compulsion to remember every word that had passed between them. As though each word was precious.

He reached for the *Times* again. Finish reading, then throw together some lunch and head for the library. He'd probably be able to acquire a temporary card. Damn, why did he still feel so tense?

He read the paper except for the business section. Out here that should be taboo. The paper stashed in a container beside the fireplace for future use, he headed for the kitchen, focused on preparing a fast lunch. Soup and a sandwich, he decided.

He settled himself before the fireplace with his lunch on a tray, grimacing as he recalled what passed for lunch in the jungle. By two o'clock, with the dishes stacked in the dishwasher, he was in the car and headed for the library.

He was impressed when he drove into the parking area. For a town with, say, 3,000 people off-season, the library was amazingly large. He left the car and walked into the two story, white stucco structure. He was always comfortable in a library setting. Books radiated friendliness, he thought. Books were a wonderful equalizer.

He smiled as the quote from Winston Churchill tickertaped across his mind: 'If you cannot read all your books, at any rate handle, or as it were, fondle them . . . Let them be your friends.'

He asked at the counter about acquiring a temporary card, was pleased that the transaction could be settled on the spot. Now he sought out the Thoreau he wanted, delighted to find it. Oddly reluctant to leave the premises, he crossed to a table at the far left of the expansive main floor and settled down to read, the sole occupant of the table.

"Hi!" An element of pleased astonishment was evident in the lilting voice that intruded on the silence. Stephie stood beside him.

"Like a homing pigeon I found my way here." His smile was casual, his pulse suddenly racing. "It's a great library."

"We're very proud of it." She shifted an armload of children's books in her arms. "It's just six years old."

"The earlier one was inadequate?" He kept his voice low out of respect for library ethics.

"The earlier one was the size of your aunt's living room. And before that, when I was in kindergarten, we had a bookmobile that came to town one afternoon a week. I think on Wednesdays."

"And you were there regularly?" he joshed.

"With my grandmother. We never missed." Her gaze was quizzical. "You said you were here during the summer? Did you see the Book Fair on the Village Green on the July Fourth weekend?"

"No, we came out later." It was as though they were totally alone on a desert island, he thought in a corner of his mind.

"My grandmother and I are there in line at ten A.M., when the fair opens. We're both drunk at seeing so many books for so little money. People come from all over the Hamptons and below. The Village Green is mobbed with people and there're special events for the little ones. Lisa loved the petting zoo. And there're home-baked goodies by volunteers. I bake cupcakes with funny faces."

"I remember book fairs when I was a kid and my parents and I went up for a month to a rented cottage in upstate New York, on the Vermont border. My parents always made sure we were there for the rash of book fairs in the area." Paul chuckled in recall. "I remember one where my mom was surprised when one of the volunteers urged her to pack the carton she was loading up more tightly. Mom said, 'Doesn't she realise the people at the pay-off table will just have to take them all out and add up the price?' Mom nearly fell on her face when she learned that that late in the day the books were sold for a dollar a carton!"

"Our first book fair — they're run by the Friends of the Library — was eighteen years ago and each year it brings in more money. This year it was over $16,000." All at once she seemed self-conscious at this encounter. "Enjoy your reading. I hope you find everything you're looking for."

"Good to see you," he said softly, wishing he

could somehow prolong this meeting. *When will I see her again? Will she be on the beach in the morning?*

Stephie hurried from the library and out to her car. Did the others at the library look at her and know how she was feeling? A stranger had come into her life and made it seem excitingly new and different. But this was insane. They barely knew each other. Yet it was as though they'd spent their lives building up to this meeting.

Go home, do the two loads of laundry waiting there. Do the vacuuming I've been postponing for three days. Pick up Lisa early. After all, this is a kind of vacation this month, before I start the second job.

She and Grandma had talked about her trying for a job at the bank, where she'd have health insurance for herself and Lisa. Dad wanted her to be free to work all three shifts from Memorial Day weekend until after Labor Day. She couldn't do that and work at the bank.

But she could work at the bank and do weekends at a shop or supermarket. Health insurance was so important. She and Lisa had nothing. Yet how could she let down the family when they needed her? She was the head waitress — she held the summer staff together.

At the house she checked her answering machine, hoping for some word from Mr Allen. No messages. What was going on with Tom's lawyer? Mr Allen had made it clear she wouldn't sign a joint custody deal. How could Tom expect that?

She went into the laundry room, threw the first batch of clothes into the washer. Lately she worried that both washer and dryer, emitting odd noises at intervals, were about to conk out. She'd bought them used — there was no warranty involved.

The phone rang. She left the laundry room and darted to pick up before the answering machine responded.

"Hello —" Breathless from rushing.

"Stephie, I was just talking to Vinnie," her grandmother reported. "You won't believe it but he said he saw Tom driving a brand new Land Rover. Where did he get the money for that?"

"Why doesn't he pay his lawyer?" Fresh anger welled in Stephie. "That's what's holding up our divorce."

"He can't afford to give you child support for Lisa," Grandma said contemptuously, "but he can dig up the down-payment on a Land Rover. A *new* one."

"Maybe he borrowed it or he's driving for somebody." Stephie struggled to be realistic.

"Vinnie said he was bragging all over town this morning about his great new car. I tell you, it's downright weird."

"Maybe somebody died and left him a bunch of money." She'd never expected child support from Tom. She hadn't seen a dime from him since their split-up. She wasn't even asking for it, though Mr Allen said she was crazy not to make it part of their divorce agreement. She just took it for granted that Lisa was her responsibility. "And if that's happened, he'll go through it like a kid with a five dollar bill at the Candy Kitchen."

Still, off the phone, she tried to fathom Tom's sudden affluence. He had made a down-payment on a brand new car but he wasn't paying his lawyer. What was that saying to her?

TEN

Paul returned to the house with a sense of being adrift. He tried to concentrate on the Thoreau, but images of Stephie intruded. Somehow, he must see her again. Just to talk with her, to be near her. It was as though all their lives till now had been leading up to their meeting — yet what could there ever be for them but a few casual encounters?

Strange how his life in this parcel of time seemed to be built around meals. He'd had breakfast at Mr John's, lunch at the house. What about dinner? Should he live it up and go to Gurney's tonight? Once last summer they'd gone to Gurney's for dinner. The food had been sumptuous, the service superb. An early dinner tonight, he decided. He'd come home and settle down to a long reading session with Thoreau.

Bring in more logs from the deck, he ordered himself. It was relaxing to coax logs into a glowing blaze. Only satin-red embers remained in the grate from this morning's efforts, a pile-up of ashes below. He dropped to his haunches before the fireplace, became engrossed in this small project. At last flames embraced each log, swept upward with an air of triumph. He stretched out on the sofa and gazed at his handiwork.

He awoke to darkness relieved only by smoldering logs in the grate. He left the sofa to cross to the avenue of sliders that faced the ocean, gazed out into early night. A sliver of moon on display. A single star. He'd promised the boys a telescope for Christmas. But Emily would take care of the shopping — despite her insane schedule she always found time for that.

He debated a moment, then reached for the phone with a sudden need to touch base with Mark and Larry. With pleasurable anticipation he punched in the numbers and waited.

"Hello, the Hamilton residence." Melinda's crisp yet cordial voice.

"Hi, may I talk to the boys, Melinda?"

"Sure, they're right here watching *Sesame Street.*"

"Oh, maybe I'd better call when their program's over." Mark and Larry's television consumption was limited.

"No, they want to talk to you," Melinda said tenderly, and he heard the usual squabbling about who was to talk first. Seniority won out. Mark poured forth minutiae about his day at school.

"Me!" Larry clamored in the background. "My turn to talk to Daddy!"

"Hi, Larry." God, he loved the kids. The best

thing that ever happened to them.

"I throwed up in the taxi," Larry reported with a mixture of excitement and regret. "So I didn't get to go to the circus. I think Seth's mommie was mad."

"Who's Seth?" He searched his mind for a connection.

"My friend from nursery school. His mommie was taking me and Seth to the circus in a taxi. But I threw up, and she took me back home. I wanted to go to the circus." An aggrieved note in his voice now.

"You'll go another time," Paul promised. "Be a good boy. I'll talk to you soon. Now let me talk with Melinda."

" 'Bye, Daddy."

"Hello," Melinda picked up.

"What's this about Larry throwing up in a taxi? Is he having an upset stomach?"

"Oh, his classmate's mother was taking the two boys to the circus and en route in the taxi Larry threw up. He seemed fine when Seth's mother brought him home."

"Could he have been carsick? But he never is," Paul said before Melinda could reply.

"I think he felt kind of insecure leaving the apartment with a grown-up he barely knows. I mean, this has been a rather traumatic period for him. Your being in the hospital for several days, and now away again. None of the three people closest to him was there and I think he was uneasy. He's fine now. It was just a brief upset.

Nothing to worry about," she comforted with confidence.

Off the phone, Paul gazed out at the night sky without seeing. Larry had felt insecure, scared, because his father had become a non-presence in his daily life. Mark probably felt something similar. The psyche of small children was so fragile, he berated himself.

I hadn't expected this to happen.

Grateful for another sun-washed day, with the temperature hovering close to fifty degrees, Stephie drove with Lisa to Dorothy's house. It always amazed her how Lisa responded to sunlit days. She was exuberant this morning, the shadowy unease that had infiltrated her much of these last few days seemingly dissipated. How did Tom have the nerve even to suggest joint custody?

As usual Dorothy offered her a cup of freshly brewed coffee. As on most mornings Stephie explained she was short of time.

"I'm hearing strange things about your ex," Dorothy confided in a voice designed to bypass Lisa, involved at the moment in greeting Dorothy's playful calico cat.

"Like what?" Stephie was instantly wary.

"He's moved back home with his aunt. It's not that he loves her company," Dorothy's smile blended cynicism with contempt. She loathed Tom, Stephie remembered. He'd screwed up on some job he'd done for her, "but it's rent free plus great meals. Still, the way I hear it, he paid her back a bunch of money she lent him."

"All of a sudden he seems to have money. I hear he's driving a new car around town." *Is he catching up with his lawyer's fees? That's important to me.*

"Yeah, a Land Rover," Dorothy said with awe.

Where was all this sudden money coming from? Had Tom conned some poor soul into giving him a bundle of money up front on some job he was supposed to do? He could do decent construction work when he wanted to but something always seemed to get in the way.

"Angie hasn't had her breakfast yet," Dorothy told Lisa. "Would you like to put this into her dish?" She extended the opened-up can of cat food.

"Yes!" Lisa reached eagerly for the can.

Stephie kissed Lisa goodbye, and returned to the car. People said one of the wonderful things about Montauk was its slow pace. So why did she always feel rushed? These past two months, especially this month, was a slowing down process for her. The summer madness was over by late September. Her hours at the restaurant shortened and this last month dinner was served only Fridays, Saturdays and Sundays. Next month she'd be in the two-job rat-race until early June. This was the time to unwind.

But how could she unwind with Tom fighting her about the divorce? No, not fighting about the divorce, she contradicted herself, fighting about how much he could get out of her financially. He knew how she had to struggle just for survival! But he was hanging on to the prospect of wheedling more money out of Grandma.

At the wheel of the car she hesitated. She was so tense, with that crazy tightness between her shoulderblades. She would allow herself a fifteen-minute walk on the beach. Vinnie could handle things without her for that little bit of time. Guiltily self-conscious, she brushed aside the thought that she might run into Paul Hamilton on the beach.

She'd hoped that Mr Allen would call last night. She'd left a message with his secretary about Tom driving around town in an expensive new car that he claimed was his. Maybe now, she thought in a burst of optimism, he'd settle down to finalizing their divorce terms. But no joint custody. No way.

Paul left the house and headed down to the beach. God, what rotten sleep he'd had last night. The last time he'd looked at the clock it was four ten and he hadn't got back to sleep after that. But maybe that was because of the naps. He wasn't accustomed to daytime dozing.

Dawn was breaking when he wandered out to the kitchen and made himself coffee. He watched the sun come up over the ocean. These were moments to be cherished. But this morning his mind was awash with torment. More than anything in this world he loved Mark and Larry but they were upset that he wasn't with them. Damn, he wasn't ready to go back to the jungle! Not yet.

On the beach he paused for an instant in homage to the grandeur of the ocean, placid this morning. Hosts of gulls rode the gentle waves. His eyes scanned the beach and then his heart began to pound. He saw Stephie striding in his direction.

All right, I know this is crazy but I need to be with her this morning. Just to hear her voice, to feel her closeness. And I know she shares this feeling.

"Hi!" Stephie waved in greeting, her smile dazzling as she moved towards him. "Isn't it a beautiful day?"

"Heavenly." He waited for her to join him.

"I should have driven straight to work, but on a day like this I couldn't resist coming down to the beach for at least a few minutes." Without her saying, he knew she'd hoped to find him here.

"I watched the sun rise over the ocean. A magnificent orange-red ball of fire." His eyes met hers. No need to explain his feelings on such an occasion. "It said to me, 'This will be a very special day'." He paused, his eyes reading hers. "Because I would come down to the beach and see you." All at once the atmosphere was supercharged.

"I tell myself this is crazy," she whispered. "I couldn't wait to come here. I prayed you'd be on the beach. That I'd see you."

"You know, don't you, that we were fated to meet —"

"I know this is a tiny, precious, parcel of time. That we'll have to go back to our normal lives . . ."

"I've never felt this way about anyone in my life. I don't want to think about moving back into the real world. I talked with you that first day and it was as though, at last, I was a whole person. You were the other half of me."

"We'll take what we can have, these precious days you'll be here." Her smile was a blend of joy, defiance and anticipation. "Tomorrow we'll worry about the rest of our lives."

He took her hand in his and they walked the short distance to his house in silence, communicating only through the pressure of their entwined hands.

While early morning sunlight filtered through a chink in the drapes, Stephie clung to Paul's shoulders as he moved above her, with her. The sweetness in his passion brought tears of pleasure to her eyes. It was as though she had never made love before. This was a wild, tumultuous experience that thrust aside all thoughts, all questions, allowing only for feeling. And then a cry escaped her, echoed by him while they clung in the final, perfect moment of their union.

"I knew it would be this way for us," he murmured, his voice husky with emotion. "Perfect. Beautiful. Like nothing ever before."

"We're out of our minds —" Her voice reproached herself more than Paul. "But it had to happen."

"I never knew I could feel this way . . ." His mouth brushed hers, moved to her throat. His hands at her breasts.

I want this to last forever. I don't want him ever to stop.

"You're wonderful," he whispered. "You teach me how to love."

And once again, so soon, she welcomed him within her. Arms and legs entangled. Two pairs of hands impatient for the touch of the other. She'd never been truly alive until now, she thought in reckless abandon.

Afterwards they lay quiescent, savoring the pleasure of their passion.

"I wish we could stay this way forever." He lay with his face pressed against hers, a leg thrown across her thighs in tender, protective embrace.

"Paul, I have to dress and head for work." Apology and regret were in her voice, in her half-smile, but reality was returning. "I'll call and explain that I had trouble with the car," she improvised. "Vinnie knows my car is temperamental."

"You'll come back to me when you're off-duty at the restaurant?"

"Until it's time to pick up Lisa at her play group," she promised.

She understood his air of urgency. How long would he be in town? Three weeks? No, less, eighteen days, she calculated. So little time to provide for a lifetime. But how many people were so enriched?

While Paul wrapped himself in a robe, she dressed and repaired her make-up, painfully conscious of the time. She called Vinnie, manufactured an elaborate alibi for her delay. Vinnie was alone in the restaurant except for the kitchen help. He hated having to fill in as waiter.

"I'll be thinking of you every minute you're away," Paul told her when they'd allowed themselves a hasty good-bye embrace. "Drive carefully. You're precious cargo."

ELEVEN

Paul forced himself to dress, overcoming an urge to throw himself back onto the bed as though the lingering warmth of her might appease the need to hold her again. He didn't want to think about a time when she would not be part of his life. She'd be back once she was off the lunch shift at the restaurant. She, too, understood how little time they would have together.

He'd never once touched another woman since the first time he and Emily had made love. He'd been so sure that Emily filled every need. But what he and Stephie felt for each other was a precious gift that touched only a few. He wouldn't think beyond each day. *Enjoy what we can share. Cherish every moment.*

All at once he was impatient to be out of the house and walking on the beach. *I'll go into town for breakfast, survive the hours until Stephie comes back to me. I want to know so much about her, about every day of all the years before we met. And yet already I feel as though I've known her always.*

No newspaper this morning. No listening to the morning news. Life would stand still until he heard Stephie's car pull up into the driveway, and he knew they could share a parcel of time until she must leave to pick up Lisa.

The sun was masked by clouds now. The ocean garbed in gray. The beach totally deserted. Leaving the house he was conscious of the blustery winds. In the distance a gull cawed in reproach. He pulled the hood of his jacket over his head, tightened it about his throat.

This was a different Montauk from an hour ago. He reached into his pocket for sun-glasses that would protect him from the sand that swept up in angry gusts. Still, he relished the challenge of combating this swift change in weather. Here was the gaunt, harsh Montauk that repelled many of the summer people. But there was an austere beauty in this 'seascape in gray'. He felt embraced in a magnificent solitude. This was his ocean, his beach. *I'm so grateful I came here!*

Stephie was glad that the breakfast crowd was light this morning, even though that meant low tips. But part of her was back with Paul. Part of her refused to relinquish the wonder of being with him. She was grateful that Gary was working on a construction job too far away to come in for breakfast.

"Juan is making French toast for you and me," Vinnie interrupted her introspection. "Maybe for once we can sit down to eat without having to get up and serve." At the moment there was no one at the counter. Stephie had provided coffee refills for the occupants of the two tables.

"Vinnie, the music is too loud," Stephie chided. The current patrons were senior citizens who, she was sure, didn't appreciate hard rock.

"So change it," he said in martyred tones. This was a familiar point of contention between them. "You'd think they'd like something to wake 'em up."

While the two of them sat down to golden French toast over which trickled the Vermont maple syrup reserved for family use, they heard the side door open. Grandma was arriving with the fresh pasta that was featured in their lunch menu, and the accompanying sauces, which she made each morning at the house.

"I had a phone call last night from Florida," Tina reported. "Your mother's pleased with the condo. Everything is clean and in working order. The same couple from last December is next door again."

"So Dad's happy." Stephie's smile was dry. She knew about the retired couple Mom and Dad had been meeting down there for the past four years. They always made Mom feel as though they were just tolerating her, though they'd struck up a warm friendship with Dad. They were loud and flashy, always on the go, Mom said. "And he's still dragging Mom all over the place with them, from morning to night," she surmised.

"You know your father," Tina sighed. "He wakes up in the morning, and if he doesn't have to come into the restaurant, it's 'What are we going to do today?' "

"When you're dead, you're dead." Vinnie shrugged eloquently. "So keep moving while you're alive. Get with it, Grandma."

"You're like your father," Tina scolded. "I don't know how Sara puts up with you."

"Hey, I know how to take care of a woman —" But he seemed relieved to be summoned to the cash register.

"I can't stay," Tina told Stephie. "There's something at the Senior Center this morning. I'll talk to you later."

By ten thirty the restaurant was deserted. The lunch regulars would begin to drift in within half an hour, Stephie surmised, enjoying this short respite. Like their father, Vinnie was restless when there were no patrons.

"Hey, I ran into that buddy of Tom's last night." Vinnie frowned in thought. "Dirk? Something like that."

"Dirk." Stephie tensed in anticipation. "What did he have to say about Tom?"

"Oh, he's got some cool job down in Southampton. With some new builder. He has to be doing great to have a car like that." Vinnie whistled in appreciation, but his eyes were speculative.

Vinnie thought she'd been a bad wife, Stephie told herself tiredly. A suspicion that wasn't new. In Vinnie's world a man could do no wrong. *'So Tom played around once in a while when he got*

105

tanked up. He always came home to you.' How would Vinnie react if he knew that Tom hadn't been just verbally abusive, that he'd pushed her around physically? Only Grandma and Mom knew about that; she'd been too proud — or stupid — to tell the men in the family.

"He won't hold that job long." Stephie knew Vinnie was waiting for some comment from her. "He never does. He's got a big mouth —" He wanted to get fired, so he could sleep till noon and carouse half the night.

"But if he does, you oughta ask for child support."

"What would be the use? I'd have to go to court every other week to try to collect." No, Lisa was her responsibility. But why didn't Mr Allen call? When would Tom sign the divorce papers? Without a joint custody clause.

"Dirk says Tom's got something going with a sexy cocktail waitress at that new bar down below," Vinnie needled.

"Vinnie, I don't care. I just want my divorce. I want to forget Tom and I were ever married."

A pair of tourists, staying at one of the few motels open year-round, strolled into the restaurant for a late breakfast. Within another twenty minutes the lunch crowd began to drift in. Stephie exchanged the usual light conversation with their regulars, but in a corner of her mind she relived joyously the brief time she'd spent this morning with Paul.

By a few minutes past two the restaurant was

106

again deserted — the off-season routine.

"You won't need me anymore," she told Vinnie. "I'll cut out now —"

"Remember, tomorrow's Friday, we'll be serving dinner weekend nights."

"I know." Her voice was sharper than she'd intended. Vinnie was pleased that he got to handle the register and keep an eye on the kitchen staff while Dad was away. Otherwise, he was the dinner waiter, along with Jeff, who worked days at a place in East Hampton. "Grandma knows she'll have to be at the house with Lisa."

She headed for the car, impatient to be with Paul. She closed her mind to the knowledge that soon he'd have to return to his other life. How could his wife insist that he stay in that awful job? Couldn't she understand what it was doing to him?

Turning into the driveway she saw Paul emerge from one of the side sliders and onto the deck. The scent of birch logs burning in the fireplace filled the air.

"Your timing's perfect." His voice was a caress. "I just put up coffee."

"I sent you a mental message." She left the car and strode to the side stairs and up to the deck, sniffing as she walked. "Two of the most heavenly aromas in the world are birch logs burning and freshly ground coffee beans brewing."

He drew her into the house, led her to the low, comfortable sofa that faced the fireplace, where a pyramid of logs blazed.

"I want to know everything about you," he said with an air of urgency. "What you were like as a little girl. What books you read, what friends you made in school —"

"Why I didn't go to college," she finished for him, allowing herself a flicker of bitterness. "Maybe if I'd been a boy my parents might have considered it. But none of my three brothers cared about school." She paused, squinting in thought. "Sometimes I wonder why I didn't just pack up and get out of town, the way some kids did once they were out of high school and with no chance of going to college. But the family needed me in the restaurant."

"You liked school," he guessed, his eyes tender.

"I loved school. I loved learning. Of course, some of the kids thought I was a nerd. You know, with my nose always in a book."

They heard the swoosh that told them the coffee was ready. Paul went out to the kitchen to pour for them. Now they talked obsessively about earlier years, relishing similar reactions to situations, the time surging past. The darkening sky reminded Stephie that she must pick up Lisa by five o'clock. She must leave in a few minutes. On impulse, determined to cling to every possible hour with him, she invited Paul to have dinner with Lisa and herself.

"That is, if you won't mind having a talkative four-year-old at the table," she added, almost shy now in offering this invitation

"I would love it," he said. But all at once he seemed troubled. "There've been so few evenings when I could sit down to dinner with Mark and Larry."

"About six thirty?" she asked. "By then Lisa will be hungry."

"That'll be great."

"I have to run —" She rose to her feet. "Dorothy expects me to pick Lisa up by five."

Driving to Dorothy's, she felt pinpricks of doubt. Would Paul think her house tiny and drab? Compared to his aunt's house it was shabby and unappealing. But they could spend the whole evening together. Just the three of them. Almost like a family.

Nobody would interrupt. Gary knew he mustn't come to the house. Grandma would make dinner for Vinnie and herself and settle down with a library book. Vinnie would watch TV. Mom and Dad were in Florida. Why not have this evening with Paul?

Her mind focused on the contents of the refrigerator. Nothing fancy, Paul wouldn't expect that. She'd start a fire in the grate as soon as she and Lisa got home. They'd never once used the fireplace at home, Dad said a fire just meant a lot of mess to clean up. Tom felt the same way. *Hey, one mistake and you'll burn the house down.*

One of the first things she'd done when Tom moved out was to call somebody to clean the chimney. In cold months she allowed herself to use the fireplace every other Saturday night. When that birch tree at the side of the house came down in a storm, Gary had brought over his chainsaw and cut up logs for her. So many of the pine trees out here were dying, but she knew not to use pine in the fireplace. One day they might even have a real view of the ocean when more of the pines went down — but it was evil to hope for that.

She frowned, remembering how Tom, after a few beers, had threatened to take his chainsaw and cut down neighbors' trees that stood in the way of their view. *'You know what that would do to the value of this place?'* The first year of their marriage he talked grandly about all the work he was going to do on the house. *'I'm a good construction worker — why not use that for us?'* But, of course, he'd never done anything except start to build a small deck — which Vinnie and Joe had come over to finish.

How would Lisa feel about having Paul over for dinner? She wouldn't be upset, would she? No. She'd liked him when they'd met on the beach that day. Lisa would feel that they were having a small party.

Paul gazed out into the night, dark and forbidding, with no trace of a moon. He didn't bother to close the drapes. Who would be on the beach at this hour? All right, a town dog or two, he conceded whimsically as he heard a bark in the distance. Perhaps a solitary jogger.

Now unease infiltrated him. Would Emily or Melinda call while he was away? But they would expect him to go out for dinner. Later — and his pulse raced at the prospect of spending the evening with Stephie — they might decide he'd driven down to East Hampton to take in a movie.

He should plug in the answering machine. He hadn't bothered before. If anybody called, the machine would pick up. He settled down to hook up the machine, recorded a message. Don't worry about phone calls, he ordered himself.

This time at Montauk belonged to him alone. Nobody would be hurt by what happened here. This was time out — a special time to help him survive the rest of his life.

TWELVE

"It's going to be a cold night," Dorothy predicted while Stephie bundled Lisa into her snowsuit. The other three little girls had already been picked up by one parent or the other. "But we've got to pay for all these nice days we've been having."

"Mommie, let's go home," Lisa urged impatiently. "I want to see the rest of *Sesame Street.*"

"We'll get there," Stephie soothed. "You'll miss only a few minutes." Dorothy was good about limiting the amount of television the little girls could watch, but promptly at four-thirty each afternoon they settled themselves before the TV set.

Not until they were nearly at the house did Stephie tell Lisa they were having a guest for dinner.

"You remember the nice man we met on the beach? Well, I invited him for dinner tonight." *Why do I sound so self-conscious?*

"He liked Chloe." Lisa nodded in approval, an expectant glint in her eyes. Remembering, Stephie thought tenderly, the few times they'd had Gary over for dinner. But then Tom found out and made rotten cracks.

In the house Stephie turned the thermostat up from the low sixty degrees of the hours she and Lisa were away. Lisa hurried to the television set, eager to continue following the antics of *Sesame Street*.

"Give me your jacket," Stephie coaxed. "Keep on your sweater until the heat comes up." Already she was questioning her impulsive invitation. But Lisa would be here. It wasn't as though she was having a rendezvous with a strange man. And who was to know?

"What are you making?" Lisa asked, her eyes glued to the TV screen.

"Just what I'd planned."

Why is my heart pounding this way? There's nothing wrong in bringing Paul here. He'll leave early, soon after I put Lisa to sleep. Nothing's going to happen here tonight. We'll just be able to see each other, talk, store up more precious hours. I don't want to think about when he goes back to the city.

"Will we have frozen yogurt for dessert?" Lisa interrupted her musing. "I want Cherry Garcia." There was a rare tone of defiance in her voice.

"Lisa, you'll have what Mommie serves." She was firm. Involuntarily she grimaced, recalling yet again the parents who came into the restaurant and allowed three or four-year-olds to make outrageous demands. Gary said it was their way of compensating for being so involved in their careers. "We'll have roast chicken because that's what I'd planned for tonight and there'll be plenty for the three of us. And garlic potatoes, which you like so much, and carrots with that orange sauce. And if you're good we'll have frozen yogurt."

She'd always worried the few times she'd allowed Tom to take Lisa for an overnight when he was at his aunt's house. Tom always gave her too many sweets, deliberately spoiled her, and Lisa would be hard to handle for the next two days. But after that night at the motel with his girlfriend she'd made it plain he couldn't see Lisa except in her presence.

Already the house was warming up, she thought, leaving Lisa to watch TV while she started dinner. With the chicken in the oven she focused on starting a fire in the grate. *This isn't a beautiful house like Paul's, but it's comfortable and friendly.*

As she'd expected, Lisa was indignant at being pulled away from *Sesame Street* for her bath.

"You'll be having dinner a little later than normal, so you need to be ready to hop right into bed afterwards." She reached into a drawer for Lisa's blanket sleeper.

"No." A faintly imperious quality showed in Lisa's voice. "I wanna wear my nightie and robe. And my bunny slippers."

"Okay. But let's run your bath now." Lisa wanted to look pretty for their dinner guest, she thought indulgently. Already, at four, she was clothes conscious.

"Lemme turn the TV loud so I can hear it in the tub."

Splashing in the tub, Lisa forgot to listen to television. She chattered about her day. She was unfamiliarly somber for a moment. "Mommie, do you love me? Really love me? Daddy says you don't."

Stephie was cold with shock. What other nonsense did he dump on their precious baby?

"Of course I love you. I love you more than anything else in this world!"

She'd put the carrots in one steamer and the potatoes in another when she heard a car pull up in the driveway. Her face luminescent, she hurried to the front door. Subconsciously she noted that it was exactly six thirty, but then she'd expected Paul to be punctual.

"I hope you're not allergic to flowers —" With a whimsical smile he held out a potted hyacinth.

"Thank goodness, no. And thank you — it's beautiful."

"Did you see Chloe on the beach today?" Lisa ran towards him in obvious welcome.

"No, I missed her today."

"I wish we had a dog." Lisa sighed.

"One day we will," Stephie said quickly. "Right now, with my crazy work schedule, it wouldn't be fair."

"We never had a dog when I was growing up," Paul told Lisa and reached to lift her in his arms. "My mom and daddy taught school, and our dog would have been all alone every day. But I'll bet

115

you see a lot of dogs when you walk on the beach."

"I'll let Lisa entertain you while I check on dinner."

Lisa was enthralled with Paul's attentions in the course of dinner, Stephie thought, and was grateful. Tom alternately spoiled or ignored her in the little time they spent together. He'd never been a real father. He'd never been a real husband. *When is he going to sign the divorce papers?*

Paul seemed to enjoy being here, she decided, while she listened to him fabricate an inventive story for Lisa.

"I like you!" Lisa declared, her smile dazzling.

"I like you, too," Paul said, serious and admiring.

Stephie brought in mugs of coffee for Paul and herself, then plates of Cherry Garcia for the three of them. She noted that tonight Lisa was taking small spoonfuls of her beloved frozen yogurt rather than her usual enthusiastic gulps. She was staving off bed-time. But already yawns took over at regular intervals.

Stephie exchanged tender glances with Paul. Being here this way with Lisa reminded him of his two boys, she sensed. He'd said he'd never been away from them overnight until he was in the hospital with pneumonia. And now again.

"This isn't a showplace like where you're staying," she said wistfully. "My grandmother teases me — she calls it my 'doll house'."

"It's a house that radiates love. The beach

house here belongs to Emily's aunt," he reminded. "On my side we were never affluent. We lived in the same small, two-bedroom apartment from the time I was two until my parents died. With the crazy housing situation in New York, nobody with a decent apartment at a fair rent ever moves. We had books spilling over, doubled up on bookshelves, so we never knew for sure what was behind the visible ones. But I never felt a lack because we didn't live in some expensive condo."

Cynicism deepened his voice. "My folks saved for our vacations each summer. Always the three of us together." His eyes mirrored painful recall. "They both died so young. But we had great summers together. And the summer I graduated high school they allowed me — reluctantly, I suspect — to drive across country with two classmates." Laughter lit his eyes now. "I'm sure they were shocked at the thought of two almost-eighteen-year-old boys and one girl of the same age traveling alone that way. But they were determined to be cool. I just hope," he said softly, "that I can be as good a parent as my mother and father were."

"I'm sure you are." Her eyes lingered on Lisa, finishing up her frozen yogurt and struggling to stay awake. "I think somebody we know is ready to go to sleep —"

"Not yet," Lisa stalled and turned to Paul. "Will you tell me a story before I go to bed?"

"Oh, I have a great one for you." He

exchanged an indulgent grin with Stephie. "But first, let me carry you to your bed and tuck you in."

"Mommie, you'll come and kiss me good-night." It was a statement rather than a question.

"Don't I always?" Stephie fought against tears. Paul was the kind of father Lisa deserved. "I'll be there as soon as I stack the dishwasher."

Once Lisa was asleep, Stephie and Paul returned to the living room.

"There's more coffee," Stephie said.

"Sit down," Paul ordered, his eyes caressing her. "I'll get it."

She hovered before the fireplace, poked at the crackling logs that lent warmth and color to the room, enjoying these moments alone to savor the wonder that she was here this way with Paul. The memory of the afternoon in his arms was etched on her brain. They both realised this could be only a brief interlude, yet this knowledge only intensified the magic of each moment they spent together.

"Coffee coming up." Paul strode back into the room, joined her on the sofa. "I can't remember when I've felt so relaxed, so happy to be alive."

"You were happy when you were teaching." How had he allowed himself to be denied that?

"It was the life I'd planned for myself since junior high." Pain lurked in his eyes, blended with frustration. "I loved working with my kids in that bad school. I brought them into my life."

Guilt joined pain and frustration. "And then I abandoned them."

"For a while you gave to them," she comforted. *Paul cares about people.* "They benefited from your being there for them."

His smile was wry. "When they'd done well, some of them, I took them to a ball game or to an amusement park. One hot day in June I took my special little group out to Coney Island. They loved it, somebody cared about them." His face tightened. "Emily told me I'd burn out. But I knew I'd never burn out."

They talked until the logs in the grate were down to glowing embers. Then Paul rose to his feet, contrite that he'd kept her awake so late when her alarm clock would awaken her early tomorrow morning.

"I didn't mean to stay so late . . ." He hesitated, then reached to pull her to her feet and into his arms. They shared a tacit pact: they mustn't make love here in this house. "This has been such a wonderful evening."

"Wonderful," she whispered.

He kissed her lightly, pressed his face against her. "Will I see you tomorrow?"

"I'll come to you after my lunch shift. Tomorrow I'll be working the dinner shift, too. But we'll have some time together." Her eyes clung to his, telegraphed her love. "Sleep well."

THIRTEEN

Paul existed for the brief interludes over the weekend when Stephie came to him. Her weekend mornings allowed for no walks on the beach, no matter how limited. On Saturdays and Sundays she went in to work earlier, dropping Lisa off at the family house en route to the restaurant, where her presence was required most of each day. He waited impatiently for the hour they could be together on Saturday and Sunday.

The instant he heard a car in the driveway he hurried out to meet Stephie, grateful for the privacy afforded by the sprawling, tree-shrouded property. With only a few words between them before they lay tangled together on the queen-sized sleigh bed that seemed designed for passion, in a world that excluded all others.

He was touched when Stephie told him that Lisa had asked about him.

"You have such a wonderful way with children, Paul. They open up to you."

She hadn't come right out and said it, but she meant that he should escape the nerve-wracking, stifling, ugly business of selling derivatives. That he should regain his self-respect by returning to teaching. She'd been upset, he understood, when Lisa told her great-grandmother about his being at the house.

"What did you tell her?" he'd asked.

"I lied. I've never once lied to Grandma before. I said that the car broke down about a hundred yards from the house, and you fixed it, and on impulse I asked you to have dinner with us. I said you were a teacher. She knows how I feel about teaching."

Why didn't her family help her to go to college? Anger welled in him. So they didn't have a lot of money — they could still manage to help her. The will wasn't there. How could they be so unfeeling? Even now, when she had Lisa, they ought to help her make the rest of her life what she wished. But he didn't want to think about the rest of her life or his. Just about *this* time. These days with Stephie.

Sunday evening he called home. He reached the answering machine. Either Mark and Larry had sleep-overs with friends and Emily was socializing, or Emily had taken them to her father's place in Pleasantville. Though she disliked her young stepmother, she wanted the boys to know their grandfather, to appreciate family.

Paul tried to settle down to read, but his mind refused to co-operate. He was painfully conscious that one week of his respite from reality was spent. A week ago tonight he had driven up to the house from Manhattan. Compulsively his eyes sought the clock at intervals. Stephie was at the restaurant. Then it would be time for her to pick up Lisa at her grandmother's. He ached to be there with her in that small, pleasant house that radiated love.

He abandoned reading early and prepared for bed, welcoming the night quiet, broken only by the sound of the pounding surf. The wind was high again, creating eerie cries in the chimney, the sky dark, foreboding. The moon in hiding. The trees beside the house bending over like exhausted old women. There'd be a storm before morning, he guessed, tossing restlessly beneath the down comforter.

Eventually he fell into troubled sleep, awoke to a gray, cold morning. Last night's storm dissipated. Snow, perhaps, in the hours ahead.

Then his mind leapt into full alert. Stephie said she'd be on the beach this morning for a short while. She'd drop Lisa off at Dorothy's, then park and come down to the beach. With a surge of urgency he hurried from bed, showered, dressed. He'd worry about breakfast later. Yesterday they'd had such a little while together. He was greedy for this morning's encounter. He remembered regretfully that Stephie had to work today. Their part-time waitress had warned she couldn't come in.

Walking down to the unblemished sand, devoid of footprints, dog prints, or the imprint of wheels, he spied Stephie walking towards him. He felt an almost overwhelming happiness.

"Hi!" Her smile was dazzling, her eyes telling

him she shared his tumultuous emotions. "Did you put in an order for snow this morning? I adore snow on the beach."

They fell into step, not daring to touch lest an unexpected pair of eyes should see them. She'd told him about the lawyer's insistence that she steer clear of male companionship until her divorce papers were signed. When was the bastard going to stop playing games with her?

"I think," he said softly, "that this is the most beautiful beach in the world. Maybe sharing that position," he conceded, "with Carmel."

"That was the beach you saw when you traveled across country with your two friends," she recalled.

"I was absolutely awed by Carmel. There was a kind of magic there, like here. I stood for an hour and watched the waves hit the shore while gulls careened over the rocks. Cormorants riding the waves." He stopped short, knowing he mustn't voice his thought that one day he'd love to show her Carmel.

Too soon she left him. Now he must push aside the hours until she came back to him. Do the routine things, he told himself. Walk into town and have a leisurely breakfast at Mr John's. After breakfast walk over to the Montauk Beach Store, the pleasant shop he had noticed earlier, and buy something for Mark and Larry. Montauk sweatshirts, he decided. Damn, he'd been disappointed not to find the kids at home last night. But he'd try again tonight, early enough so they would be awake. It was incredible how much he missed them.

The morning dragged because this was time stolen from being with Stephie. But she'd be at the house a little past two. She'd promised to bring a photograph album from the family house. He felt a towering need to permeate his memory with visions of her as a little girl, as a teenager. He was envious of those years before she came into his life.

Ignoring the raw cold of the day, he paced the deck at the approach of two o'clock, impatient to be with her, to hear her voice, to hold her in his arms. Then he saw her car coming down the road. He hurried down the side stairs to meet her. She emerged from the car with an armful of what appeared to be scrapbooks.

"I'm sorry to be so late. We had a heavy lunch turnout — I couldn't get away." Her eyes were soft with apology. "And I can't stay long. We have an early dinner party of twenty-four. A couple celebrating their sixtieth wedding anniversary. Vinnie will need me."

Damn, why couldn't the dinner party have been last month? "You brought the albums." He forced a smile, reached to take them from her.

"I'll pick them up tomorrow and return them. I told Grandma I was feeling nostalgic and wanted to spend the evening after Lisa goes to sleep just looking at all the snaps again." He sensed an inner debate in her. She was wishing she dared invite him to the house, but she was afraid. She was still waiting to hear from the lawyer about her divorce papers.

"You'll be off tomorrow," he said tentatively. "Could we spend the day together, somewhere away from here?"

"Yes," she effervesced, her smile rebellious. "I'll take you to a wonderful bird sanctuary near Noyack. This time of year there'll be nobody there except us. The trees are gaunt and bare. I'll bring birdseed, and they'll come and eat from our hands. Some will be shy at first, but then they'll see the others eating away, and they'll get brave. Paul, it's such a beautiful experience."

"I'll love it."

Too soon, Stephie declared she must return to the restaurant.

"We don't often get these dinner parties, especially at this time of year. Vinnie and Dad have been moaning for weeks about how slow business is." She chuckled. "They cry every winter, but the restaurant manages to survive."

"I'll sit here all evening and pore over the albums," he told her tenderly. "I have to catch up on all those years."

"I'll be here early in the morning. We'll have breakfast together."

"I'll miss you." He held her close for a moment, then released her. "I'll dream about you tonight."

Paul stood at the slider wall and stared out

into the darkening sky, lulled into serenity by the stillness, unbroken except by the waves caressing the beach. Why couldn't time be locked into place? He never wanted to leave here. And yet at the same moment he felt a need to touch base at home. He'd never been separated from Mark and Larry this long. And what had happened to Emily and himself? Where had they gone off-track? But he knew the answer to that: when they began to worship her father's gods.

He checked his watch. Mark and Larry should be home now. He'd missed them last night. Try again. Without bothering to turn on a lamp — the only illumination in the room the glow from the constantly-burning logs in the fireplace grate — he crossed to pick up the cordless phone, settled himself in a corner of the sofa and dialed.

"Hello, the Hamilton residence." Melinda's clipped British voice was oddly reassuring.

"Hi, Melinda. How's everything down there?"

"Emily took the boys out to Pleasantville yesterday," she reported. "They came back loaded down with new toys. You know how their grandfather spoils them. Emily said she thought she'd be home fairly early tonight —"

"Are the boys there?"

"Coming right up. All right, stop fighting," she scolded them. "You'll both have time to talk to your daddy."

"Daddy, I'm talking first," Mark said in triumph. "Melinda says Larry has to have his face washed while we talk."

"I hear you had a good time yesterday." Why did he always feel defensive whenever he thought of his father-in-law?

"It was okay. Daddy —" Mark sounded troubled. "When are you coming home?"

"Soon." He tried to sound casual. He didn't want to think about going back. "Hey, you're a big boy now — you're in the first grade. You can handle this."

"Daddy, are you and Mom getting a divorce?"

"No." The sharpness of his reply startled him. "Wherever did you get that idea?"

"I dunno. I thought maybe — like some of the other kids . . ." Mark's voice trailed off.

"I'm out here to rest up," he told Mark. "Mommie and I explained that to you." Several of Mark's young friends shuttled between apartments — one night with the mother, the next with the father. They lived like gypsies, he thought in distaste. "Tell me about school today," he ordered. Here was safe ground.

Why did Mark ask if Emily and he were getting a divorce? Kids were so quick to pick up vibes. Was it something Mark heard Emily and her father discuss? Was the husband always the last to know?

FOURTEEN

The atmosphere in the restaurant was convivial. Stephie and Vinnie moved about the tables with bright smiles. Stephie paused at intervals to cuddle the seven-month-old-granddaughter passed from arm to arm in the course of the evening. Most of the guests were extended family. Four generations at the tables. Stephie knew most of them.

Her mom and dad celebrated their silver wedding anniversary seven years ago, she remembered. How had Mom put up with Dad all these years? But then, hadn't they expected her to stay married to Tom? What was it Dad said when she told him she was divorcing Tom? *'When you get married, it's for keeps. What the hell's the matter with young folks these days?'*

Grandma said, *'For the children you stay together — if it's possible.'* With Tom it wasn't possible.

Stephie heard the phone ring. Vinnie was picking up.

"Hey, Stephie, it's for you," he yelled over the noise.

She hurried to the phone. "Who is it?" she asked Vinnie.

"Chuck Allen," he told her, with raised eyebrows. "It must be important if he calls you this late."

She reached for the receiver. "Hello."

"I called you at home and got your machine. I figured you'd be at the restaurant. I heard about the anniversary bash."

"What's up?" She tensed in anticipation.

"I had a conference with Tom's attorney this afternoon. Tom says he's ready to sign the papers, even though he thinks your settlement offer is too low. But he's made some stipulations." A wary quality in his voice now.

"Like what?"

"He still insists on joint custody. He wants a guarantee that you won't move more than a thirty minutes' drive from Montauk, and —"

"I told you. I'll never agree to joint custody! Tom knows that." She was trembling now.

"His attorney hinted that he might drop the cash settlement if you agree to joint custody."

"I won't allow him to have joint custody. Not even overnight custody. You know what happened the last time he had Lisa overnight!" Tom was only making these demands to get back at her! After an hour with Lisa he was bored. "I'll agree to his taking her for Saturday afternoons or Sunday afternoons." She was struggling for calm. "I'll forget about child support." To get support she'd have to be in court every other week anyway. She'd manage somehow.

"I'll talk to his lawyer," Allen said. "But we're

not dealing with a logical man."

"I know that." He still couldn't get over not falling into money when he married her. "But we can't go on like this forever. Tom has to understand that."

Stephie tossed restlessly most of the night. Her mind churned with Tom's outrageous demands. Why had he stopped yelling for a larger cash settlement? How could he afford to drive a new Land Rover? Vinnie said it was probably a lease, that his new boss must have lied to the financing people about how long he'd been working for him.

"What do you want to bet he'll lose the car in less than two months?" Vinnie had scoffed. "Everybody knows he never holds a job for more than a few weeks."

The first hint of dawn was in the sky when she at last drifted off to sleep. She grimaced in reproach at the raucous intrusion of her alarm clock little more than two hours later. She reached to silence it, staring into the semi-darkness for a few moments. Then all at once joy surged in her. This was her day off, to be spent with Paul.

Lisa didn't understand she wouldn't be going to work today, yet Stephie felt guilty that she was stealing this day for herself. Sometimes on her days off she took Lisa to her play group after lunch and used the afternoons for all the chores that piled up during the rest of the week. But this was like no other time in her life.

She hurried to raise the thermostat, returned to her small bedroom to prepare for the day. She paused to glance out a window. The morning was faintly overcast, only an occasional blob of blue pushed through, but the high winds of yesterday had subsided. A good day for visiting the Wildlife Refuge.

Paul stood beneath the shower spray and willed himself to relax. Soon Stephie would be pulling up into the driveway. They'd have breakfast together and head out for a full day that belonged to themselves alone. He wouldn't think about anything else. Yet, in truth, his brief conversation with Mark yesterday evening ricocheted in his mind. 'Daddy, are you and Mom getting a divorce?'

Had he been blind? Was Emily unhappy with their marriage? Had Mark overheard Emily and her father discussing this? He and Emily had little time together these past three years — ever since he went into the company. But he'd thought she accepted this as part of their building for the future, even while he resented it. He'd thought she loved her job but just a few days ago she'd said, 'Sometimes I wonder what I'm doing in this insane business'.

He brushed aside introspection. A car was coming down the road. Stephie? He turned off the water, emerged from the stall and reached for a bath towel, listening to the sounds of the car while he hastened to dry himself. Yes, it was Stephie, he decided with elation. He wrapped himself in a plaid wool robe and strode from the master bathroom, across the bedroom and into the hall, calling ahead.

"I'll be right there, Stephie —"

She waited at the side door with an effervescent smile. "Am I too early?"

"You could never be too early." He drew her into the house. "Coffee's ready. I put it up before I went into the shower." His eyes held hers, glorying in what he read there. "I remember when I was about nineteen, I had this roommate at college who insisted it was decadent to make love in the daylight."

"Then let's be decadent." Her anticipation matched his own.

His arm about her waist, he prodded her into the bedroom. The bed was still rumpled, as though in welcome, he thought while he helped her out of her clothes, then allowed his robe to drop to the floor. "This is the closest I've ever been to heaven."

Afterwards they lay tangled together, her head on his shoulder, both drowsy, content, shutting out the rest of the world.

Stephie stirred, for the moment uncertain as to her whereabouts. Then she felt the weight of Paul's leg across hers, and her face grew tender. They'd both fallen asleep. With care not to awaken him she disengaged herself, left the bed.

She'd make breakfast, then call him. But moments later, while she dressed, he awoke.

"What did I ever do to deserve you?" But the somberness in his eyes refuted the lightness of his voice. He knew this was only a fleeting interlude.

"You may not say that when you eat my breakfast. Do you have fruit in the house?"

"Always. Bananas, oranges, apples, blueberries. What are you conjuring up?"

"My special pancakes. I'll start right now. But you can have coffee while you're waiting." Keep the mood light.

While she mixed the batter for the pancakes, added the fruit, brought out the griddle, he stood by admiringly, sipping fresh-brewed coffee. Yet she sensed he was troubled. But not until they'd devoured a shocking number of pancakes and were sipping from refilled coffee mugs did she voice what darted about in her mind.

"Something's happened to upset you," she said gently, her eyes questioning.

"I talked to Mark last night." He stared into his coffee mug. "It was a disturbing conversation. He asked me if his mother and I were getting a divorce."

Stephie froze, her mind in sudden chaos. The implication was unnerving. She gazed at him and sensed his unhappiness. "You don't want that to happen to your kids," she said after a moment. Yet for a tumultuous instant she'd visualised a world where she and Paul could be together for the rest of their lives.

"I see how some of their friends shuttle between parents — it scares me." But she saw the hunger in his eyes for a life shared with her.

"During the summer I go into New York two or three times a month. To buy items for the restaurant. I go in on the Hampton Jitney. At least twice each summer I see some little boy or girl as young as six or seven traveling alone. One parent puts a child on the Jitney to be met by another parent at the other end. I've sat holding the hand of one little boy who cried all the way into Manhattan. I stayed with others at the 39th Street Jitney stop for up to an hour until a parent arrived to claim his or her child."

Paul winced. "A little kid alone in mid-Manhattan — that's a terrifying picture. Thank God, you were there to be with them."

"I swore I'd never allow Lisa to face a situation like that. It's bad enough that Tom's fighting for joint custody right here in town. But he'll never get it!" Her eyes glowed in defiance. "I'll pack up and run away in the middle of the night before I'll let him have custody of her."

Only now did she bring herself to tell him what had occurred the night when Tom brought Lisa — and his current girlfriend — to his motel room.

"Tom's a stupid, vindictive man." She struggled for calm. "But he won't win. I won't allow that."

"What about that wildlife refuge?" He tried to

dispel her somber mood. "Have you decided not to take me there?"

They left the house in Paul's white Mercedes.

"I've never been in a Mercedes before. Of course, the two most popular cars in the Hamptons are Mercedes and Jaguars." Laughter lit her voice. "When I was in high school and my friend Diane was out for the summer we used to count the Mercedes and the Jags at the Bridgehampton Commons and on the parking lot at the East Hampton A&P. And we'd figure how much money sat there."

"My father-in-law thought it was important I drive a Mercedes," Paul said wryly. "To indicate to my clients that I was a success."

"I would have felt a huge success if I could have gone to college and then come home to teach — and drove a 'pre-owned' car." Laughter lit her eyes. "I love the way 'used' cars have been renamed 'pre-owned' cars."

The morning continued gray and gaunt. On other occasions such weather would affect her mood, but not now. Not when she could rest her head this way against Paul's shoulder. Yet at intervals she felt a tightening in her throat. It was impossible to erase from her mind Mark's question to his father. *'Daddy, are you and Mommie getting a divorce?'* Paul had been shaken, yes, but she knew that he was conscious of what that could mean in their lives.

Stephie leaned towards the window as they approached the small pond at East Hampton, as always commiserating with the swan who skimmed the water.

"He looks so lonely," she mourned, and for an instant Paul's gaze left the road. "Until about two years ago there were two swans there. I keep wondering what happened to the other one, and why a companion hasn't been brought for him."

"Maybe he's a misanthrope."

"I don't think so," she contradicted. "Why doesn't he have a friend?"

"A lover," Paul said softly. "I wonder how many other people — romantics like you — have asked themselves the same question?"

"A lot," she guessed. "East Hampton attracts romantics as well as the rich."

"When do we turn off Route 27?" he asked, moving one hand from the wheel to rest on her knee.

"At the sign that points to Sag Harbor. It's just ahead."

Is Paul's wife thinking about divorcing him? Would he be upset? Would he be relieved? Can there be a life for Paul and me beyond these precious weeks?

FIFTEEN

At Sag Harbor, striving for a casual mood, Stephie suggested a brief sightseeing tour. "The summer people have gone — it's a great time to see it."

"Then let's do it," Paul approved.

"We'll park and walk a bit." *Is he upset that his wife may be thinking about a divorce? Is he anxious about how it would affect his sons?* "Sag Harbor was settled in 1730 and was a whaling center back in the mid-1800s. You must see the marble monument in the Oakland Cemetery. It's marble, carved like a broken mast with a smashed whaleboat and a dead skipper and — But you have to see it to feel its impact."

Stephie forced herself to concentrate on showing Paul highlights of the charming village. They paused before the three-storied American Hotel, admired its ground-floor porch with graceful, Gothic revival columns. She showed him the Whaler's Church, built in the style of an Egyptian temple — the most impressive building in the town.

He listened absorbedly while she told him the history of the large Greek revival structure that was now the Whaling Museum, and pointed out the array of historic houses. But all the while her mind struggled to deal with the dizzying thought that there might be a life ahead that they could share.

They stood at the wharf, in its winter garb, and imagined how it must have been two hundred years earlier.

"We just drive over the bridge there." She pointed, in a corner of her mind telling herself that this was a day she would remember forever. "We make a left at the blinking light — that takes us to the Wildlife Refuge."

They drove in a cozy silence to their destination. Hand in hand they walked from the car into the 187 acre Morton Refuge. The trees were tall and bare, their trunks close together. They followed a narrow, beaten path until Stephie decreed they should halt. Birds flitted among the branches. A pair of raccoons scampered at their feet. Gesturing for silence, Stephie reached into a pocket of her jacket and withdrew a bag of birdseed.

"Just hold the seed in your hand, outstretched this way," she whispered. "They'll come to us."

It was always a magical moment when, at last, the first bird came down from a bough to eat from her hand. Then another and another — and then both she and Paul were deluged by eager eaters. She looked up at his face and knew he shared her sense of awe at standing here this way. She smiled tenderly as he coaxed a more audacious bird to allow a shy little one to approach and nibble.

They seemed frozen in time, she thought, both enraptured by this experience. A faint drizzle descended from the darkening sky, threatened to become stronger.

"We'd better head for the car," she said, half-apologetically.

At Paul's suggestion they decided to drive into East Hampton for lunch. They parked, left to stroll the now uncrowded streets, clogged with pedestrians four months earlier.

"I love East Hampton this time of year," Stephie confessed. "When the crowds have gone. Most of the shops are still open — and the galleries. Once in a while in the winter months, when the weather is grim, Grandma and I run down to catch a movie. Of course," she added with laughter, "I want to be sure I'm back home in Montauk by bedtime."

"Where shall we have lunch?" Paul asked. "I'm famished. All this clean sea air!"

Stephie chose a restaurant where she felt she would not run into people she knew. The tab was high but she knew Paul would not be worried about this. They contrived to be seated in a secluded corner where he could hold her hand under the table without their being observed.

"I've never been here," she whispered, "but everyone says the food is superb." This was a part of the East Hampton she knew only from

Dan's Papers, the haunt of the entertainment world's celebrities.

Entering into the spirit of their gregarious waitress, they ordered with an air of adventure. This was a world away from Bertonelli's Oasis, she mused. But she and Paul were not a world apart. They came together as one whole. *Can there be more for us than these three weeks?* She suspected that Paul, too, was trying to deal with this thought.

Paul talked again about Carmel. "It sits there on the rugged coastline in the midst of towering Monterey pines and cypresses. The ocean seethes, beating against the rocks. Stevenson wrote about the changing color of the water, the thunderous sound of the ocean pounding the shore. The sand, white and beautiful. You'd love Carmel, Stephie —"

Does he mean that someday we may see Carmel together? Can that ever be?

They lingered over lunch, loathe to destroy the mood that enveloped them.

"I want to go shopping," he told her. "I want to buy a lovely necklace for you. I need to know that something of me is close to you every moment of the day and night."

"Something silver," she said whimsically, "so that I can wear it in the shower. Wear it while I sleep." *Can my whole life turn around because Paul is here? Can there be a tomorrow for us? A lifetime of tomorrows?*

They strolled about until Paul chose a shop for

their small venture. Almost immediately she spied a silver chain with a pendent depicting a seascape.

"Can you engrave on the back of this?" Paul asked the charming saleswoman.

"Just tell me what you'd like." She smiled confidently, offered him a scrap of paper and pen.

Stephie leaned forward to read the words he was printing on the paper: 'How do I love thee? Let me count the ways —'

In her mind she continued the Robert Browning poem: 'I love thee to the depth and breadth and height / My soul can reach . . .' Her face was luminous. She should have known Paul would know the poets. Her father, her brothers, Tom — to them poetry was something absurd, unmanly. Tom's pickup truck was his poetry, she thought with contempt.

The saleswoman explained that the pendant, with the engraving, would be ready anytime on Monday. Paul glowed. She sensed that he'd contemplated adding 'Paul' after the quote but reasoned this would be injudicious. *But not if he's free.*

"We'd better head back for Montauk," she said wistfully when they left the shop. "I have to pick up Lisa."

Paul stood on the deck and watched while Stephie drove away. Belatedly he remembered that she had forgotten to take the family photo albums with her. But she'd get them tomorrow.

He clung to the knowledge that he would see her tomorrow.

This would have been a perfect day if he'd been able to block out those few minutes on the phone last night with Mark. Mark had stirred up thoughts that were foreign to him. Disturbing. *Where am I going with my life? How can I go back to that endless nightmare?*

Why was it always he who called home? Emily hadn't called once since he'd come out here.

Night came so early this time of year, he thought, staring out into the darkness. The ocean was rough, pounding against the beach. He felt a surge of loneliness that only Stephie could have eased. As though to reach out to her, he walked to the over-sized coffee table where he'd placed the photograph albums she'd brought for him to see. He dropped into a chair to pore over the snapshots where she appeared.

Reluctantly he closed the last of the albums and considered dinner. Again he'd settle for something here in the house. He was in no mood for a solitary dinner in a restaurant. He hesitated, then reached for the phone. He'd talk to the kids, reassure himself that they were all right.

"Hello." Emily's voice greeted him.

"You're home early —" He hadn't meant to sound harsh.

"I do come home early some nights," she shot back defensively. "You sound as though you're disappointed to find me here."

"Just — surprised," he said lamely. "I know your crazy schedule."

"How are you?"

"Okay. It's very quiet and peaceful here. I don't listen to the television, don't read the newspapers —" He paused. "How're the kids?"

"They're all right. Do you want to talk to them?"

"Sure." *She's anxious to get off the phone — she doesn't want to talk to me.*

Again, the usual battle between Mark and Larry about who would talk first. As usual, Mark won.

"Hi, Daddy. When are you coming home?" The routine question.

"Soon," he promised. "Tell me what happened at school today."

Mark reported on his activities with an exuberance that seemed tainted with defiance. His best buddy had become the enemy. Now Larry was clamoring for his turn, and Emily intervened to mediate. He talked for a moment with Larry, then the phone call was over. Emily had come on for a moment to say that Melinda warned the boys' dinner would get cold if they didn't come to the table. Emily had probably just come home to change for some social event, Paul interpreted. She was scarcely aware of his absence, he taunted himself.

Guilty that she had spent a day off without including Lisa in her activities, Stephie allowed herself to be persuaded to read yet another story.

"Just tonight," Stephie stipulated. "Now lie back and listen —"

Before she'd finished the first sentence, she saw Lisa's eyelids begin to droop. The second sentence and she was fast asleep. Stephie leaned over to kiss her, tucked the covers around the small shoulders and tiptoed from the room, closing the door behind her.

She was debating about whether to sit down and write out checks for bills that were due or to defrost the refrigerator when she heard a car turn into the driveway. She went into the hall and switched on the outside lights, curious about who might be arriving. She saw her grandmother's beat-up station wagon. Grandma hated to drive at night. What had brought her out? In a flurry of alarm she thrust open the door.

Tina Bertonelli emerged from the car and headed for the house. "Is Lisa asleep yet?"

"She drifted off a few minutes ago." What was Grandma carrying?

"Oh, I wanted to see her face when she unwrapped this."

"What is it?" Stephie reached for the huge carton.

"A present for her from Gary. It's the biggest teddy bear she's ever seen."

"That was sweet of Gary." But Grandma didn't come over just to bring the teddy bear.

She was smiling, but her eyes were anxious, Stephie thought.

"They don't come better than Gary."

"Gary said he's working right now on a house in Riverhead. That's why he hasn't been in the restaurant for breakfast." She didn't want to think about Gary. Not now.

"Let's have coffee," Tina said casually. "Vinnie went over to Sara's for dinner. I just made something fast for myself, didn't bother having coffee. I figured I'd have it with you."

"Lisa will be out of her mind when she sees this." Stephie deposited the carton in a corner of the living room. "Let's go out to the kitchen." What was on Grandma's mind? She was stewing about something.

Not until the coffee was up, and Lisa's bedroom door closed lest they awaken her, did Tina open up.

"I was talking on the phone with Ethel Latham just before dinner. She said she saw you in East Hampton today. With a man." Questions in her eyes.

"I was with Paul Hamilton. We drove down there for lunch. He's staying in Montauk for a while at his aunt's house." *How can I explain to Grandma how I feel about Paul?*

"That's the man that you had to dinner?"

"That's the one." *I know — I'm out of my mind. He's a married man, with kids. My divorce is hanging in the air.*

"Do you think that's a good idea?" Tina was

striving to sound casual, but Stephie felt her anxiety. "I mean, considering how nasty Tom is about the divorce. All he needs to go off the wall is to think you're seeing another man. He's already mad that you're going out with Gary."

"Paul will be in town just another two weeks, not quite that." How could she expect Grandma to understand what Paul had come to mean to her — and so fast?

"Gary's a good man. You know he's serious about you. He's so fond of Lisa. Stephie, I worry about you."

"Because Ethel Latham says she saw me in East Hampton with a man?" She fought for calm. "That's the bad part about living in a small town. Everybody minds everybody else's business!"

"Stephie, don't see him again. It'll mean trouble."

"He's leaving in two weeks. I'll never see him after that."

"Stop seeing him now," Tina pleaded.

"I can't," Stephie whispered. "He'll be here for such a little while." *Grandma, I can't not see him.*

SIXTEEN

Paul awoke early after a night of broken slumber. He lay in the early morning darkness, gazing at the ceiling without seeing, in his mind reliving the previous day. He felt again his reluctance to part with Stephie when it was time for her to pick up Lisa.

I hate the evenings, they seem so desolate. But Stephie's afraid to have me at her house — that one dinner invitation was given on impulse. Her crazy husband would make life even more miserable if he knew about us. Hell, they've been separated for two years!

What prompted Mark to ask if Emily and I are getting a divorce? Did he hear something? Or is it just that he sees classmates shuttling between parents? It's so common these days.

In a surge of discomfort Paul thrust aside the comforter, left the bed. He couldn't deal with such problems at this point. He would just handle one day at a time.

He crossed to open the window wall of drapes, gazed out at the pink-streaked sky. It was going to be a beautiful day. He was up early enough to see the sunrise, though a glance at the clock told him it would be a while yet.

Determined to banish troubling thoughts, he ordered himself to shower, dress, put up coffee. He'd be on deck to witness the sun rise over the ocean. And after that he'd have a tiny parcel of time on the beach with Stephie. Then he'd wait for her to come back to him when she was off duty at the restaurant.

Don't think beyond today.

Stephie drove with Lisa to Dorothy's, dallied a few minutes, then hurried to meet with Paul. Still silently fretting over last night's encounter with her grandmother. She'd thought it was unlikely that anybody she knew would see them in East Hampton. But that was wishful thinking. Would Ethel Latham spread the word around town that she was down in East Hampton with a strange man? Everybody knew she was fighting for a divorce from Tom.

Would Tom hear about it? He knew she'd been going out once a week with Gary, and he was furious about that. This would incense him even more. One of the summer people — a man who drove a Mercedes, she thought with shaky humor.

But I mustn't spoil the time I can have with Paul by worrying about what Tom might think. For a little while Paul and I can live in a special world of our own.

Yet at truant moments, simultaneously frightening and glorious, she asked herself if there

148

could be more for Paul and her than this stolen interlude.

In a tacit pact Stephie and Paul concentrated on seizing every possible moment together, both frustrated by the need to spend their evenings apart. At intervals in the days ahead she debated about asking Paul to come to the house for dinner with Lisa and herself. Each time she forced herself to discard this thought. Each day she read questions in her grandmother's eyes, felt her anxiety.

On Saturday, after an afternoon of exploring each other's thoughts, glorying in this venture, Stephie prepared to leave.

"So early?" Paul protested.

"I have to pick up Lisa and take her to Grandma's," she reminded. "I can't just dump Lisa and run." Her smile was rueful.

"I wish there was a night when we could be together from sunset to sunrise," he said passionately. "I feel bereft when you walk out and I know I can't see you until the next morning."

"I know," she whispered. Each parting carried a note of urgency.

"Could you — just once —" The atmosphere was electric. His eyes searched hers. "Stay the night?" She knew he meant, 'Can you come back to me tonight?'

"I might — I might ask Grandma if Lisa can stay with her until morning." She paused, took a deep breath. Grandma would understand the reason for this request. Would she agree? "Mom and Dad are down in Florida. Vinnie would think nothing of it — there've been occasions when Lisa slept over with Grandma." No one except Grandma need know. "I'll talk to her. It would be so wonderful —"

Her heart pounding, she drove Lisa to the family house. Again, the question ricocheted in her brain: was Paul's wife contemplating a divorce? Was his marriage over? There was no doubt in her mind that Paul loved her as obsessively as she loved him.

"Mommie, did you see Chloe this morning?" Lisa broke into her thoughts.

"Not today, but I saw her yesterday. She had a friend with her. A chocolate Lab."

"I wish we could have a dog." Lisa uttered her frequent complaint with a melodramatic sigh.

"Darling, someday we'll have a dog. Right now we'd have to leave him alone too much. I wouldn't want him wandering around town alone."

"Chloe does," Lisa said triumphantly.

"But that's not good. When the time is right, we'll have a dog."

At the family house Lisa was settled, with a fresh-from-the-oven chocolate chip cookie, before the television set to watch her favorite video.

"I can't stay long," Stephie reminded Tina. "We have the 'early bird special' now." But she was searching for the words that must be said. Grandma would be shocked that she would behave this way. She knew Paul was married, had two sons. Technically Stephie was still married. But how could she deny Paul and herself this precious gift? Their advance Christmas present.

She waited until she was sitting with Tina in a corner of the kitchen with Lisa in sight but beyond earshot before she broached her question.

"Grandma, could Lisa sleep over with you tonight? She always likes that so much." She was stammering before the accusations in her grandmother's eyes.

"Stephie, this isn't right," Tina said quietly. "You'll only be hurt."

"We have such a little time." Stephie's eyes pleaded for understanding. "I can't deny us this. Paul's like no one I've ever known. We complement each other in every way. I need this for all the years ahead."

"Gary will be a fine husband, a loving father to Lisa. Don't sell him short." Tina was upset.

"Paul will be leaving in another week — I'll never see him again." But she clung, in a corner of her mind, to the thought that Paul's wife might ask him for a divorce. Not knowing about Paul and herself, making this decision without involving them. His wife's own independent decision. "Grandma, let us have tonight."

"I'll take Lisa with me to church in the morning," Tina said. "Then we'll come to the restaurant for brunch. She'll love that."

151

"Grandma, I love you," she whispered, her face radiant. "I brought Lisa's nightclothes and fresh clothes for tomorrow —"

"You know you can twist me around your little finger." Tina's tone was light, but her eyes were grave.

Paul sprawled on the sofa, willed himself to read. But his will was weak. Would Stephie be able to come back tonight? Stay the night? Let us have that much, he thought defiantly.

The phone rang. He tossed aside the book, reached for the cordless phone that lay on the coffee table.

"Hello —"

"Paul, it's all right," Stephie whispered. "I should be there about nine."

"I'll be waiting." A joyous anticipation swept over him.

"I have to go now." She hung up. Paul understood. No one must know.

Too restless to read, even to sit, he paced about the room, crossed to the wall of sliders to gaze out into the night. He should call home, talk to Mark and Larry. It was unlikely that Emily would be home tonight. She was obsessed by the need to 'keep up contacts, make new ones,' her father's mandate for success.

Why was he the one who phoned home? Emily never called him. She didn't want to talk with him. That came across loud and clear.

Does Emily want a divorce? Emily and I were two

different people six years ago. She'd loved her career but it wasn't all-consuming then. Where did we lose our way? We're out of touch with each other.

He was conscious of an urgent need to talk to Mark and Larry. He didn't want them to join the cadre of children who commuted between parents. But Emily and he had allowed a wall, an insurmountable wall, to rise between them. If Emily wanted a divorce, did he have a right to deny her? And yet guilt tightened a knot about his throat. A divorce would give him freedom to spend the rest of his life with Stephie.

Don't think about that tonight. Let the next dozen hours be unspoiled by anguish or guilt. These hours belonged to Stephie and himself.

No, he wouldn't call home and talk to the kids. He would take a long walk on the night-dark beach, with the ocean a lulling symphony. And then he'd come back and wait for Stephie to arrive.

It was almost nine o'clock when Stephie pulled into Paul's moon-splashed driveway, where the air was fragrant with the scent of logs burning in the living room fireplace. Instantly the outside lights bathed the area in brilliance. He'd been waiting for her.

"Since you're a chocoholic, I brought chocolate mousse cake for a late snack," she called as she darted towards the stairs.

"Admit it," he joshed. "You're as mad about chocolate as I am." He moved down the stairs in his impatience to greet her. "But I'm more mad about you."

"Don't squash the cake," she warned, lifting her face to his. Tonight they'd brush aside everything except the pleasure of being with each other, she told herself, and read this same resolution in his eyes.

They made love with obsessive abandon. Afterwards, exhausted, Stephie allowed Paul to wrap her in a designer robe he'd discovered in the master bedroom closet but which was four sizes too large.

"You look like a little girl in her mommie's clothes," he teased.

They sat before the living room fireplace, where smoldering logs lent warmth and color to the room, and gorged on chocolate mousse cake.

"The logs reflect my mood," he mused. "Content just to be . . ."

"Mine, too . . ."

"Tell me again about when you were a little girl and went to the bookmobile with your grandmother," he ordered.

"You know all about that," she protested.

"Tell me again."

They talked far into the night, exploring each other's souls. They made love again, and fell asleep tangled together. And then — far too soon — the alarm clock rang. And reality set in.

The dream was over, Stephie taunted herself. It was time to return to that other world. She gazed for a poignant moment at Paul, still asleep despite the alarm. Get up, dress, go in to the restaurant, prepare for the Sunday morning church-going crowd. She gathered up her clothes and disappeared into the elegant master bathroom. When she emerged, she saw Paul, wrapped in his bathrobe, standing by a slider and gazing out into the dusky morning.

"Did my shower wake you?" Her heart was pounding. One week from today he would take his gear down to the car and begin the trek back into Manhattan. When his eyes met hers, she knew his thought mirrored hers.

"I turned around in my sleep and you weren't there — that woke me up."

"You were sleeping so soundly. I thought you'd sleep for hours."

"Don't leave me just yet," Paul pleaded. "Let's go out on the deck and watch the sun come up over the ocean."

"I'll be late," she hedged.

"It'll be coming up in a few minutes." He reached for her jacket, sprawled across a chair, and held it for her. "Please —"

For a moment his arms closed about her as she reached to zip her jacket against the morning cold.

"You'll freeze on the deck," she protested.

"I won't even notice. But first let's go to the back of the house." He prodded her down the hall. "There's something you have to see."

At a rear slider they gazed out through gaunt, thin boughs to the magnificent view of a near-full moon that seemed painted against a dusky sky.

"Oh, Paul, how beautiful!"

"And in a couple of minutes we'll see the sun rise over the horizon. Do you wonder that I love Montauk?"

Why couldn't I have met Paul eight years ago, before I made such a mess of my life by marrying Tom? How are we to survive without each other?

SEVENTEEN

Stephie walked with compulsive swiftness to the restaurant. She was relieved to see the tables still unoccupied, only a pair of regulars at the counter. It would be at least an hour before people began to stream in for Sunday breakfast.

"Hi!" Donna, their part-time waitress, who worked weekends and covered for her on her days off, greeted her with a nervous smile. "I thought the weather was supposed to warm up. I almost froze coming in."

"It's cold," Stephie agreed. But sensuously warm in the restaurant.

"Stephie, I told Vinnie — I can't come in tomorrow. I have to take my kid down to Southampton Hospital for some tests. You know, more of her allergy problems."

"I'll come in." Stephie struggled to hide her disappointment.

"I'll be in Tuesday for sure, though," Donna promised.

"Stephie, I want to talk to you," Vinnie called from the kitchen.

"Just let me hang away my coat." What did Vinnie want to talk to her about? He couldn't know about last night — could he?

She hung away her coat, walked into the kitchen. Vinnie was waiting for her in a far corner where they could talk in private.

"What is it, Vinnie?" Guilt was giving way to alarm.

"Gary's all right, but Tom dragged him into a fist fight last night."

"Oh, Vinnie —"

"I heard about it from one of the guys who broke up the fight, then from Gary. He's all right," Vinnie soothed. "He's got a black eye and some bruises. He tried to call you this morning to tell you before the word spread around town. He didn't want you to worry about him." A question in Vinnie's eyes.

"He must have called when I was walking on the beach," she alibied. "My answering machine wasn't on. Why did Tom do that?" she asked in mounting exasperation.

"Why do you think? Tom can't stand to believe you've found somebody else."

"He's an animal." But poor Gary — such a sweet, gentle man.

"I warned Gary. Until your divorce comes through, he'd better cool it."

"He knows that." She was unconsciously sharp.

"Oh, Mom called last night from Florida. Before I got home." He sounded self-conscious, Stephie thought. He'd probably stayed over at Sara's. "She spoke to Grandma and Lisa.

158

Grandma said Lisa stayed over so they could go to church together this morning."

"Lisa likes to do that every now and then." Stephie tried to appear casual. "They'll come in for brunch later."

This was going to be such a long day. No way she could see Paul this afternoon. Lisa would be here at the restaurant until Grandma took her home for her usual early dinner. Paul knew that. He'd be so disappointed that she had to work tomorrow. *I'll be disappointed.*

On Monday morning Stephie hurried to Paul after she'd taken Lisa to Dorothy's. She was still upset about the encounter between Tom and Gary. She shouldn't come to Paul's house this way — they should meet on the beach, as though just in a casual encounter. For the first time she admitted to herself that she was physically afraid of Tom.

"I have coffee waiting." Paul reached to pull her close. "I'll make breakfast for us and —"

"I have to go to work," she broke in.

"I thought you were off today —"

"The woman who fills in for me can't make it. But she'll come in tomorrow — we'll have the whole day together." Her eyes radiated a blend of apology and joyous anticipation. Yet she knew that Paul, too, was conscious of how little time remained for them. Unless his wife asked for a divorce. *The decision must be hers — both she and Paul understood that.*

"You'll have time for coffee," he said, prodding her towards the door. "But what rotten luck."

"I'll be clear after the lunch shift," she reminded. "I'll come then."

"We'll have most of tomorrow," he said urgently. "Nobody will take that away from us."

Paul prepared breakfast for himself, ate without tasting. No sunrise to watch this morning. Heavy gray clouds hung overhead, reflected in the water. The waves tumultuous, crashing against the sand.

He poured a second round of coffee in his mug, returned to the table. What was he to do with himself until Stephie came back? Walk on the beach. That was part of his therapy. Then drive down to East Hampton to pick up Stephie's necklace. With a need for action, he cleared away the breakfast dishes, brought down his jacket, checked its pockets for gloves and ski cap. All right, hit the road.

For almost an hour he walked on the windswept beach, deserted except for a cluster of seagulls. Some of the tightness between his shoulderblades had eased, he noted subconsciously, as he left the beach and headed for the car. Traffic would be light at this hour of a December morning. None of the bumper-to-bumper traffic of July and August.

Driving down Main Street he was conscious this morning of the imminence of the holiday season. Christmas wreaths adorned each of the elegant new lamp-posts of which Montauk residents were so proud. Christmas trees lined the sidewalks. Wreaths flanked the gazebo on the Village Green. Shop windows, too, reflected the holiday season.

There was a Christmas spirit in small towns that Manhattan seemed to lack, despite the famous Christmas tree at the Rockefeller Center and the fanciful shop windows at the likes of Lord & Taylor and Saks. Growing up in Manhattan he remembered gazing out their apartment windows to see colorful Christmas displays in opposite windows. Now people seemed too busy to bother.

He noted with approval the Christmas displays on view along Route 27 to East Hampton. The night scene would be spectacular. Mark and Larry would love it, he thought, and was conscious of a discomforting desolation.

In East Hampton he parked and headed for the gift shop. East Hampton never totally lost its resort aura, and he remembered what Stephie had said: 'I love East Hampton this time of year, when the crowds have gone. Of course, I want to be sure I'm back home in Montauk by bedtime'.

The saleswoman who'd sold him the pendant greeted him with a warm smile. She knew how he and Stephie felt about each other. Only she knew.

"The engraving's done." She reached beneath the counter for a box, opened it to reveal the necklace. "Please check that we've got it right."

Paul reached for the necklace, turned over the pendant to read the words engraved there: 'How do I love thee? Let me count the ways —'

"It's fine. Thank you."

He rejected the offer of a bag, slid the box into his jacket pocket and left the shop. Outside the shop, while their mother inspected the contents of a window, a pair of small boys romped with a black Lab pup. The dog of choice in the Hamptons, he thought humorously, and now there was a Lab pup in the White House.

All at once Paul felt a twinge of loneliness. He hadn't seen Mark and Larry in over two weeks, the longest he'd ever been separated from them. And again Mark's question echoed in his mind: *'Daddy, are you and Mom getting a divorce?'* Had Mark overheard something he wasn't meant to hear? Was Emily working herself up to ask him for a divorce? Clearly she wasn't happy.

The tables at The Oasis were emptying. It had been a good day for a Monday, Stephie thought. Some weekend people were staying over, going back this afternoon. She'd be able to get out in another thirty or forty minutes. She was impatient to be with Paul, to be sitting before the ever-burning fireplace with his arms around her . . .

"Stephie —" Vinnie's voice was sharp.

"What is it?" She hurried behind the counter to where he stood staring out the window.

"There's Tom in his Land Rover." A touch of envy in Vinnie's voice as they watched him emerge and head across the street. "He's coming here." Vinnie turned almost accusingly to Stephie. "Did you ask him to come?"

"No." She tensed in wariness. Mr Allen had warned her not to discuss the divorce with him. *'Let his lawyer talk to me.'* Was he coming to talk about his fight with Gary? He can't know about Paul.

She geared herself for a confrontation. Where did Tom get the money to buy or lease a Land Rover? Was some bank stupid enough to give him a huge loan on the strength of the new job he bragged about? She glanced nervously about the dining area. Please God, don't let him start an ugly scene here.

The door swung open. Tom swaggered inside.

"Hi, baby." He startled her with his exuberant air. He waved to Vinnie, turned to her. "Do you know what today is?"

"Monday, December 15th." Her voice was faintly acerbic.

"Hey, you don't remember?" he clucked. "It's my birthday!"

"Happy birthday," she said drily.

"My aunt's makin' a special dinner tonight. She — we — thought it would be right for Lisa to be with us. She's bakin' a chocolate birthday cake because she knows Lisa likes chocolate."

"Who'll be there?" Stephie was uneasy.

"Just Aunt Alice and me. 'Course, it'll be late

163

when we've eaten and cut the cake and all, so Aunt Alice thought Lisa should sleep over and I'll bring her home in the morning."

"No." Stephie was blunt. "Bring her home by nine o'clock."

"Come on, it's my birthday."

"You bring her home by nine o'clock." Stephie's eyes met his in defiance. "I won't have her sleeping over."

"You're a little bitch," he hissed, too softly for the remaining diners to hear. "I'll pick Lisa up at Dorothy's at five."

"I'll phone Dorothy and tell her it's all right." Let him know *she* was in charge of Lisa.

"Do that."

Exuding rage, he stalked from the restaurant.

EIGHTEEN

Stephie waited impatiently for the last diners to leave, for the restaurant to close, replaying in her mind the disturbing encounter with Tom. She'd phoned Dorothy, told her that Tom would be picking up Lisa today. Lisa would be fine — Tom's aunt would be there.

At last Vinnie hung the 'Closed' sign on the door. She hurried out to the car with a sense of urgency. It had always been this way with Tom; she'd never known when he'd erupt into an ugly scene. And how awful for Gary, to be attacked that way.

Why am I allowing Tom to take Lisa for the evening? He knows, after that last nasty business, that he's supposed to see Lisa only in my presence. That much Mr Allen accomplished. If she's not home by nine o'clock, I'll get a court order against him.

She drove into Montauk. In a few minutes she'd be with Paul. She needed to feel his arms about her, to hear him reassuring her that Lisa would be all right.

"You're upset," Paul said when she walked up the stairs to the deck. "What's happened?"

Haltingly, with his arm about her while they

walked into the cozy warmth of the house, she told him about Tom's latest demand.

"His aunt will be there," Paul soothed. "Lisa will be fine. She may eat too much birthday cake," he said with an attempt at humor, "but she'll be all right."

"I'm scared," Stephie admitted.

"There's no need to be. Are you cold?" he asked solicitously, because she seemed to shiver for a moment.

She managed a wisp of a smile. "I won't be in a few moments."

"Let me close the drapes —" He kissed her, a gentle, promising kiss, and went to the slider wall.

Paul's right. What can happen to Lisa when Tom's aunt is there?

Paul came back to her and she abandoned thought. For a little while they'd be in their private Eden.

"When I found you," Paul said much later, with Stephie nestled in his arms before the smoldering fire, "I found the other half of myself."

"I never suspected life could be so beautiful," she whispered, the firelight bathing her in rosy color. But soon — so soon — it would end, her mind tormented. Unless — But she mustn't think about that.

"You're beautiful. Body and mind and soul."

"I wish we could stay this way forever." She reached to touch the pendant that hung about her throat now, engraved with the words that were a haunting love song. But reality intruded. "I'll have to leave in a few minutes."

"Why?" He was startled. "You said Lisa wouldn't be home until nine o'clock."

"I should be there in case something happens — I mean," she stammered, "if Lisa decides she doesn't want to stay and Tom has to bring her home. I wish I could stay — but I mustn't."

"We'll have tomorrow."

"All ours." Her face radiated her joyous anticipation.

"I'll call you later," he decided impulsively. Other evenings he hadn't called because that was time that belonged to Lisa. "That's all right, isn't it?"

"But we can only talk for a few minutes at a time," she stipulated. "In case Lisa wants to talk to me. I don't have 'call waiting'." A tiny luxury she couldn't afford.

"Three minutes on, three minutes off," he decreed, chuckling. "But first, tell me your phone number!"

The house felt strangely empty without Lisa, Stephie thought in the intervals between phone calls. But when Paul's voice came to her it was almost like being with him. They ate their dinners while they talked. Paul reported small incidents of his childhood that remained in his memory. She recalled poignant incidents in her childhood that she had never shared with anyone else. But her eyes strayed to her watch, and she was apprehensive.

"I know it's ridiculous of me," she apologized, "but I need to drive over past Tom's house. Just to know he's not having some wild party —"

"You'll feel better," he comforted. "Call me again if you can."

Stephie put down the phone, went to the hall closet for her coat. The phone rang. She rushed to answer.

"Hello?"

"I just talked with Vinnie." Her grandmother's anxious voice came to her. "He told me about Tom and Gary. Darling, you have to make Gary understand that he has to keep his distance until your divorce comes through."

"I haven't been seeing him, Grandma —" Just when he came to the restaurant for breakfast.

"I've been thinking — maybe if we up the settlement, Tom will stop playing these awful games. I have that lot out in Hither Hills that I can sell. I meant to hang on to it to leave to you and the boys, but —"

"Grandma, Tom isn't talking settlement anymore." She felt a tightness in her throat. "He just wants to punish me with this joint custody deal."

"I don't like the way he's suddenly running around town in that Land Rover, flashing fifty dollar bills."

"He sold somebody a big story about his wonderful contacts in the construction field," Stephie surmised. "He's got a good job and was able to lease the Land Rover. And the fifty dollar bills — he's probably got two or three that'll be gone in a few days. Like his job," she predicted with contempt. "He talks great but he never delivers."

"Stephie, are you still seeing that man from New York?"

"He's leaving the end of the week." *I don't want to think about that. Will there be a small miracle that'll keep us together?* "Did Vinnie tell you that Tom has Lisa for the evening? It's his birthday and —"

"Vinnie told me," Tina broke in. "His aunt is there — he'll have to behave himself. Alice is a decent woman. Weird, sometimes, but decent."

"I want to drive by just to convince myself he isn't throwing a wild party. I'll talk to you later, okay?"

"Go drive by the house," Tina said compassionately. "But I'm sure it's just a quiet dinner party for Tom and Lisa and his aunt."

Stephie left the house and went to the car. A bleak, cold evening with the wind shrill and foreboding. Few cars on the road. The town in its night garb.

She slowed down to a crawl at the stretch of road where Tom's aunt lived. Already Christmas lights outlined the windows of the modest white clapboard house and its front door and adorned a small pine on the front lawn. In the driveway sat Tom's recently acquired Land Rover. And his aunt's ancient station wagon. Not a wild party, she told herself in relief.

Vacillating about the wisdom of calling home, Paul finally capitulated, impatient to hear the sound of the boys' voices. They'd still be awake — it wasn't too late to call. He could hear the ringing at the other end, but nobody responded. It was a Monday night, he thought in a flurry of alarm. Mark had to go to school in the morning, Larry to his nursery group. Where the hell were they?

"Hello —" Emily's voice came to him, sounding annoyed at this intrusion. He remembered her impatience with telecommunications people who invaded privacy at all hours.

"Hi." Paul was relieved at hearing a reply. "How's everything?"

"I'm furious," Emily said. "I have an important meeting tomorrow morning, and Mark comes home with a note from school. I'm to be there between nine thirty and ten A.M. to discuss some problem."

"What kind of problem?" Mark was a laid-back kid, he got along well with everybody.

"They didn't say. Why must it be then when I have this meeting at ten sharp?"

"Call up and postpone it. What the devil could be so important? Mark's all right, isn't he?" he asked in fresh alarm.

"He's not sick, if that's what you mean." Exasperation lent sharpness to her voice.

"Call up the school and explain about your meeting," Paul urged. Many of the mothers of the kids at the school were professional women. The staff should understand. "What could be so serious?"

"If I don't show up, or try to cancel, then I'll be the uncaring, delinquent mother." Emily uttered a beleaguered sigh. "I'll go."

"Can I talk to Mark and Larry?" he asked after a moment.

"I don't think that would be a good idea." A guarded quality in her voice now. "You just confuse them. They talk to you, then they're upset. Paul, I have to go. Melinda's calling me."

Off the phone Paul sat immobile, in mental chaos. *What does she mean — I just confuse them? I don't talk to them about divorce. Mark picked that up from her. And what's more important, a business meeting or Mark?*

If I was teaching instead of being imprisoned in that rotten investment banking jungle, I could spend so much more time with the kids. But Emily and I sold out. Mark and Larry are being shortchanged because of their parents' professions.

Walking into the house, Stephie was conscious of an aching emptiness. Lisa wasn't here. But she'd been overly suspicious, she rebuked herself. Tom was celebrating his birthday with just his aunt and Lisa. With a sense of relief she went to the phone and called Paul.

"It's all right," she said. "No wild party."

"Lisa will be back home soon," he comforted.

"Probably falling asleep on the way."

"Tom didn't say a word about the divorce when he came to the restaurant. Just the business about his birthday." He'd called her a bitch when she'd refused to let Lisa sleep over. "But maybe his lawyer told him not to talk to me."

Is Paul's wife preparing to divorce him? I mustn't think about that. Like Paul said, we have to live each day as it comes along. But by next week this time he won't be here.

They talked for almost an hour without interruption.

"Paul, I'd better get off now. Tom should be bringing Lisa home any minute. But tomorrow's ours," she reminded him tenderly. "I'll be there early."

She reached for a magazine, tried to focus on reading, tossed it aside after a moment. She was too tense to read. It was almost nine. Was Tom waiting for the last minute to bring Lisa home? That would be like him.

She began to pace. Her eyes sought out the clock at brief intervals. It was nine o'clock. Why weren't they here? She crossed to a window facing the street, gazed outside. Not a car in sight. Only a cat darting across the road. She debated about phoning the house, but she didn't want to talk to Tom's aunt. His aunt still thought it was terrible that she wanted a divorce.

It was 9:05, then 9:10. Not a car on the road.

What was Tom trying to do to her? Now it was 9:14.

If Tom doesn't show up with Lisa in another few minutes I'll call the cops.

NINETEEN

At intervals of two or three minutes Stephie's eyes swung to the clock above the fireplace. *Where are Tom and Lisa? Why hasn't he brought her home? He was supposed to bring her back by nine o'clock!*

Now it was 9:32. Call the cops. No, her mind rejected. Not yet. Call Tom. Grandma always scolded her for over-reacting. But Lisa was not going to sleep over, she told herself defiantly. No matter how hard Tom's aunt tried to persuade her.

She darted to the phone, punched in Alice's number.

"Hello," Alice's voice greeted her.

"Hi, this is Stephie." She tried to sound casual. "I was wondering if Tom had lost track of the time. It's way past Lisa's bedtime —"

"Oh, they left already. They should be there any minute." A coldness in Alice's voice that telegraphed her disapproval. Right now Alice was basking in Tom's seeming affluence, Stephie thought, but it wasn't long ago that she threw him out for sponging off her.

"Thanks. I'm sorry to have disturbed you." Belatedly she remembered that in the eyes of

Tom's aunt only rude, uncivilized people phoned after nine o'clock in the evening. "Good-night."

No need to panic, her mind exhorted. Tom's aunt said they'd be here any minute. But heart overruled mind. Where were they?

She crossed to the window and stared out into the night. Relief surged in her as she saw a Land Rover approaching. It was slowing down. Tom was late — but he was bringing Lisa home.

She hurried to the front door, pulled it open. Tom was carrying Lisa.

"She fell asleep in the car," Tom said, walking into the house. "I'll put her in her bed."

Stephie followed him to Lisa's bedroom. She'd just put Lisa into her nightgown and let her sleep, she thought tenderly. She leaned over to switch on the night light, though she doubted that Lisa would wake up until morning.

"Hey, we made a cute kid," Tom drawled, closing the door to the bedroom behind them. "We did somethin' right." He reached out for her hand.

"Tom, it's late. I have to be up at six."

"You're still damn good-lookin' —" There was an amorous glint in his eyes as he pulled her to him.

"Tom, let go." Her eyes flashed fire.

"You're still my wife," he reminded.

"No," she said bluntly and pushed him away.

"You're an uppity bitch!" he flared.

"Tom, go." All at once she remembered with

painful distaste the night he'd physically attacked her while Lisa stood screaming in her crib. "Just get out of here." She was cold and trembling.

"I'm going," he shot back. "I don't need you. I can get better just by snapping my fingers. But you'll pay for being so snotty to me." He paused, his face exuding a blend of contempt and triumph. "I'm not asking for joint custody. I want full custody. You're an unfit mother!"

Pale with shock she stood immobile while he stalked to the door and out of the house. What did he mean?

Paul thrashed about the bed willing himself to sleep, but his mind rejected this. He remained as wide awake at midnight as at midday. Had Emily expected him to offer to drive into town and meet with Mark's teacher in the morning? Physically it was possible. He could drive to the city, talk with Mark's teacher, then drive right back out here.

Tomorrow might be the last full day he could ever spend with Stephie. How could he deprive himself of that? She'd been so upset when she last called, terrified when Tom got nasty and talked about demanding full custody. The bastard was grandstanding with that garbage about her being an unfit mother. No mother could be more devoted to a child than Stephie to Lisa. He was just doing that to delay their divorce.

Truantly the prospect of Emily's demanding a divorce infiltrated his thoughts. He could never make such a move himself — the importance of family was too ingrained in him. He didn't want to see Mark and Larry torn between himself and Emily. But suppose Emily insisted?

Fighting demons, he pulled on his jacket and went out onto the deck. The sky was a dark canopy, devoid of moon or stars, the wind sharp and shrill. The waves hit the beach with Wagnerian fervor. Gradually, standing here and gazing into the night, he felt the tightness at the back of his neck and between his shoulderblades diminish. Maybe now he could sleep.

The alarm rang off. Stephie reached to silence it. In a moment she would get up, go out and raise the thermostat. The wind had howled all through the night. It would be cold and gray — no beautiful sunrise this morning.

She was conscious of an aching tiredness. She'd slept little last night. She'd been haunted by Tom's accusation that she was an unfit mother. That wasn't true!

She'd tried to bury in a corner of her mind an inchoate fear that Tom knew about Paul and her. Grandma had heard about it from Ethel Latham. How many other people had Mrs Latham told about seeing her in East Hampton with a strange man? Was that why Tom talked about asking for full custody?

She tossed aside the comforter and slid from

the bed into the dank cold of the early morning. She would get Lisa ready for the day, give her breakfast and head for Dorothy's. Today belonged to Paul and her.

Each night gave way to day so late this time of year, Stephie mourned, while she prodded Lisa from the house and into the car. The sun never rose above the horizon this time of year until past seven and this was one of those December mornings when fog settled heavily over the town, lending an eerie atmosphere with visibility hardly more that forty feet.

"Mommie, I'm sleepy," Lisa said reproachfully.

"Put your head against me and nap while we drive," Stephie cajoled. "And if you want to sleep at Dorothy's, she'll put you into a bed and you can sleep." But she felt painful guilt that she had not allowed Lisa to sleep later. And she felt a touch of relief that Lisa didn't realise this was her day off. *Was she being a bad mother?*

"I had two pieces of birthday cake," Lisa said with sudden triumph. "It was all chocolate, inside and outside."

"Did you have a good time?"

"Yeah . . ." But there was a hint of doubt in her voice.

"Close your eyes now and take a little cat nap," Stephie encouraged.

"What's a cat nap?" Lisa asked, but already she was drifting off.

Lisa was sleeping soundly by the time Stephie

pulled into Dorothy's driveway. Again, guilt imprisoned her. She should have allowed Lisa to sleep late this morning. She was putting her own wishes ahead of what was good for Lisa. *She was not being a good mother.*

But five minutes later Lisa joined a small friend in watching Bugs Bunny on television, and Stephie left. The fog was beginning to dissipate. Driving was less of an effort. Yet, pulling into Paul's long driveway, she subconsciously glanced about to make sure no other car was in sight. Later she'd call Mr Allen and tell him what had happened last night with Tom.

"You look tired," Paul greeted her tenderly. "You didn't sleep well last night."

"How could I?" She managed a wistful smile.

"Let's go out to the kitchen and I'll make breakfast for us." He reached for her hand. "The fog's lifted. We can see the ocean now."

"You're so good to me," she whispered.

"You haven't seen my omelets yet," he boasted goodhumoredly. "If ever I'm stranded and need a job, I can make it as a short-order cook in some small-town diner."

"You make the omelets, I'll put up the coffee." It felt so good just being here with Paul this way.

While he dealt with their omelets, Paul told her about summer trips with his parents to Canada when he was an early teenager, fighting to divert her from troubling thoughts, she understood.

"Dad liked to pile into the car with us and drive without reservations anywhere. He figured we'd always find motel units that were available. But Mom had this yearning to stay at the Hotel Frontenac in Old Quebec City and every summer for three years we drove up in front of that magnificent old chateau with such expectations. And always we discovered there wasn't an inch of space available."

"My grandmother always talked about taking me to Italy to show me where she lived when she was growing up but there just never seemed to be the right time. She lived in a village at the foot of the Italian Alps. She said the views were spectacular."

"Was she in Italy during World War Two?"

"Oh, yes! There was an American soldier billeted in her house, like in all of the houses in the village. She's never stopped talking about how wonderful he was to her family, bringing them food and blankets from army headquarters. She said people there loved the Americans. I think that's when she fell in love with the prospect of living in this country. She came here with her husband and my father just three years after the war." *I wish Grandma could know Paul.*

"It's wonderful to be part of a big family like yours." He knew about her aunts and uncles and cousins, all of them to be here in Montauk for Christmas. "I never knew any of that. My mother and father were both an only child and I

180

was *their* only one. I used to be envious of friends who sat down at Thanksgiving and Christmas at a table that had to be extended to banquet size to handle everybody."

"Grandma's cooking up a storm already." Stephie laughed in recall. "Lisa tries to wheedle her into taking out some cookie dough from the freezer and baking it now."

"I remember Mark's first Christmas. He was too young to understand the Santa Claus routine, but we dragged him to Macy's to sit in Santa Claus's lap. And we bought toys as though toymakers were about to become extinct."

"Lisa can't wait for the Christmas tree to go up at Grandma's." *I don't want to think about Christmas. Paul will be back in that other world of his. Won't he?*

"Omelets coming up. Toast ready. What about the coffee?" Paul contrived an almost festive mood.

"I'm pouring." For a little while, here with Paul, she could forget the world outside.

While they sipped at coffee and Paul talked about a hiking trip along the Appalachian Trail with a high school buddy, Stephie debated about calling Mr Allen. He ought to know about Tom's latest threat.

"You're worrying again." Paul's eyes were compassionate.

"I was thinking I ought to call Mr Allen, my lawyer. To tell him about Tom's newest craziness." She glanced at her watch. "He should be in his office any minute now if he doesn't have to be in court."

"Call him," Paul said gently. "And then we'll plan our day."

"I'll try his office —"

At the kitchen phone she waited expectantly. She was about to decide he hadn't arrived when Allen's voice came to her.

"James Allen's office. Allen here. Good-morning."

"Mr Allen, this is Stephie." Her words tumbled over one another in her haste to report on last night's encounter with Tom. "He was so angry. He insisted he'd ask for full custody. He'll never get that, will he?"

"I see no grounds for that," Allen said with an air of irritation, then hesitated. "Stephie, you haven't been indiscreet, have you?"

"No!" But her heart was pounding. Could Tom know about Paul and her? Was he going to drag that into their divorce? "You know how ridiculous Tom is. He's angry because I rejected him — he's vowing to get back at me."

"I'll try to reach his lawyer and find out what this is all about. I'll get back to you."

"Let me call you," she said quickly. "I'll be running around on errands today. Shall I call in a couple of hours?"

"Make it around noon," he said. "I have a meeting with another attorney this morning. I should be clear by then."

She put down the phone, stared into space.

No way would she ever let Tom have even partial custody. *Not even if I have to run out of town in the middle of the night. Tom will never have custody of Lisa.*

TWENTY

Paul waited for Stephie to speak. What had she denied so explosively? Why was she so distraught?

"Stephie?" He punctured the painful silence.

"I have to call Mr Allen back around noon." She paused, seeming in some inner battle. "He — he asked if I had been indiscreet." Her eyes implored him to deny this.

"You haven't lived with Tom for two years." Paul kept his voice even. "No judge in his right mind would object to your seeing another man." That was what frightened her, wasn't it? That Tom might know about them.

"I can't get his words out of my mind." She closed her eyes as though to escape this ugly recall. "He said I was an unfit mother. He said he was asking for full custody."

"He'll never get it." He left the table to go to her. "Your lawyer knows that."

"But why did Mr Allen ask me if I — I had been indiscreet?"

"The routine question so he knows what he has to deal with," he comforted, pulling her close. He felt her heart pounding against him. He knew the one way to distract her. "You're not thinking about that. This is our day." Gently chiding now.

"I won't let him have custody of Lisa!"

"That won't happen. He's just trying to frighten you." He lifted her face, brought his mouth down to hers. In just a little while she'd forget about that bastard of a husband. Together they'd move into that world that excluded all others.

Her head on his shoulder, their arms about each other, they walked into the master bedroom. The drapes were drawn. The only sound that of the waves crashing against the beach. Their symphony, he thought, while together they sought their way to their private Eden.

They lay tangled together, loathe to separate. These were precious moments, he thought, made more precious by the realization that their time together must soon end. Yet unwarily he asked himself, "Can there be more?"

"I love you so much," she whispered. "I never thought I could love anyone this way —"

"The way I love you." He brushed a stray tendril of silken hair Tom her forehead. "To be able to love this way is a very special gift."

"I felt so guilty this morning when I woke Lisa. On my days off I've always let her sleep late if she wants to. But I couldn't today."

"Stop feeling guilty," he ordered. But his mind spewed out the knowledge that Emily had been summoned to Mark's school. What was happening to Mark? Were he and Emily bad parents?

"Let's go for a walk on the beach," Stephie said with a touch of defiance. "That can't be considered indiscreet."

"Let's." He pressed his face against hers. "But first more coffee. You know I'm addicted."

"I'll put it up. As soon as I'm dressed."

Paul was all at once conscious of the time as he sat with Stephie over coffee. By now Emily would have talked with Mark's teacher. She'd go into the office. He would call her, find out what was so terribly important that she had to be there at nine thirty this morning.

"I'm going to buzz Emily," he told Stephie. "Mark's a six-year-old. What could he have done that required a parent's being dragged to school?"

He called Emily's personal line, braced himself for what he might hear.

"Emily Hamilton." She managed to sound simultaneously warm, confident and efficient.

"What was the big deal at the school?" He tried to sound indulgent.

"Oh, God, they're weird!" She grunted in distaste.

"Like what?"

"His teacher complained Mark has been acting out in class. The school psychologist implied that it was a 'cry for help'. That something is missing in his home life." Her voice was unnaturally high-pitched. "She suggested that

186

we consider family therapy. I'm afraid I wasn't very diplomatic —"

"Are they throwing Mark out of the school?" he asked in alarm. "A first-grader?"

"No, they won't do that." Cynicism crept into her voice. "Not with what we're paying to keep him there."

"I'll call tonight and talk to him," Paul began. Forgetting for the moment her refusal to let him talk to Mark and Larry last night. "Explain to him that —"

"No," Emily broke in. He heard her take a deep breath, an indication she was struggling for poise. "Paul, I told you last night I don't think your phone calls are good for Mark. Don't call," she emphasised. "It just upsets him. Wait a sec —" He heard her in conversation with her administrative assistant. "I have to go. But don't call Mark. Please don't do that to him."

He heard the phone click at the other end. He sat immobile, trying to digest what he'd just heard.

"Paul?" Stephie leaned forward solicitously.

"Emily talked with Mark's teacher and the school psychologist. They said Mark has been acting out in class. They've decided something's missing in his home life, that we ought to go into family therapy. They're talking about a little six-year-old." His mouth tightened. "I said I'd call and talk to Mark tonight. Emily gave me strict orders not to. She said my calls just upset him."

187

"He's a little confused. He —"

"The inference was that we're bad parents but Emily interprets that to mean *I'm* a bad parent."

"I'll never believe that."

"I can't deal with this now." He reached for her hand. "This is our day. Let's go for our walk on our beach."

"And later," she decreed, "we'll have a picnic on the deck. The sun's breaking through the clouds. It's going to be a lovely day after all." Her eyes defied the elements to decide otherwise.

Stephie was pleased that the beach was deserted except for a pair of black Labs and a host of seagulls riding the waves. *What if someone sees Paul and me walking on the beach this way? That means nothing. We could have just met and struck up a casual conversation.*

They walked in silence for a while, content just to be close. Both conscious that they must not appear to be lovers. Paul asked her about the houses high on the cliffs. Stephie related what she knew, then told him about the magnificent 'cottages' designed by Stanford White.

"We'd better turn back," Paul said. "It's a long haul."

"Our beach, our ocean." Her smile was dazzling. "But we grant visitation rights to the gulls and to the town dogs."

"I can agree to that." His eyes made love to her, though they would not to touch in public.

They began the trek back. Paul told her about a three-week vacation on Cape Cod the summer he was twelve.

"That was the summer of my major sunburn. Mom kept telling me to cover up, but at twelve you think you're invincible. She stayed up with me most of the night ministering to that awful burn."

"I've sat on a log on the beach this time of year and felt the sun burning my legs right through my slacks. My mother tells me I'm out of my mind." She laughed softly. "Grandma says, 'Just don't sit there too long'."

"Your grandmother sounds like a very special lady."

"She is," Stephie said softly. *Oh, I wish Grandma could know him.* "When we get back to the house, I'll drive over to the IGA and pick up picnic makings. With all this walking we'll be hungry early."

"I'll go with you."

"That wouldn't be wise. Not when Tom's searching for something to make me look bad in court."

"I found an electric grill in the closet off the kitchen." Again Paul was making an effort at lightness. "Does that give you any ideas?"

"Oh, yes." She picked up his mood. "Chicken cutlets with that secret sauce of Grandma's. You'll have to close your eyes while I make it."

"I'm not sure I can do that. How can I endure not seeing you every moment we're together?"

"Try," she urged. "Well, peek a little."

I could never be silly this way with Tom — he'd think I'd lost my mind.

By the time they returned to the house the sun was brilliant, casting a golden sheen across the water. They made a festive event of preparing for lunch. With the grill on the deck, along with a small bistro table and matching chairs, Stephie headed for the IGA to shop. While she was gone, Paul promised, he'd set the table and put up coffee. Stephie was ever conscious of a layer of desperation beneath their conviviality. *Our time is so short.*

Arriving back at the house, relieved that she had encountered no one she knew in the IGA, Stephie heard the noon siren go off. Time to call Mr Allen. All at once she was tense again.

She deposited her IGA bag on the kitchen table, lifted her mouth for Paul's light kiss.

"It's phone call time again," she said with a wry smile. Paul was still fuming over the call to his wife, she thought, despite his light banter. "Mr Allen said he'd be in his office by noon."

"I'm sorry. Mr Allen isn't back yet," his secretary apologised a moment later. "May I have him call you?"

"I'll try again in thirty minutes. Okay?"

"Sure. I'll tell him."

Stephie made a lively production of preparing the sauce while Paul monitored the chicken cutlets on the grill. But all the while her mind was in turmoil. Was it just Tom's threat of the moment to demand full custody of Lisa? Or was he so vindictive he'd try for that?

The sun lent an amazing warmth to the temperature on the deck and there was little wind. It could have been an early spring noon rather than only eight days until Christmas Eve, Stephie thought, while they lunched on grilled chicken and the salads she'd picked up at the IGA.

"This isn't December," Paul joshed, reading her mind. "It's mid-April and early flowers are bursting out all over."

His smile was beguiling, his voice high-spirited, but his eyes betrayed him. Stephie knew he was upset that his wife had told him not to call home, not to talk to Mark. He knew his marraige was on shaky ground.

"I'll get our coffee." He pushed back his chair, rose to his feet.

"I'll try Mr Allen again."

"Stephie, it's going to be all right," Paul insisted. "There's no judge on earth who'd take Lisa away from you."

"I'm so scared. You don't know Tom. He's capable of such awful things."

"He won't get total custody," Paul reassured her again.

While he poured coffee into over-sized mugs, she phoned Allen's office again.

"James Allen's office. Allen here." His secretary off to lunch, Stephie pinpointed. "Good-morning. Or rather, good-afternoon," he added good-humoredly.

"Mr Allen, have you talked to Tom's lawyer?"

"We had quite a long talk," he said with a wariness she'd come to recognise as bad news. "Tom's brought his account up to date. And yes, he's going to ask for full custody."

"On what grounds?" Outrage blended with shock and terror in her voice. "He's out of his mind!"

"He's claiming that you've been having affairs with other men. That you even had sex in Lisa's presence. We'll have to prove he's lying —"

"Of course he's lying! There's never been anything more than a few casual dinner dates with Gary. You know about that —"

"He's got three men who're willing to go to court and say that they slept with you at your house. That on two occasions Lisa was in the same room. We'll have to check out those dates and —"

"He's dragging in his weird buddies!" she broke in. "Not one of them has ever set foot in this house!"

"We'll have to disprove them," Allen pointed out cautiously. "They'll give us dates. You tell me where you were those nights." He paused. Again, wariness in his voice. "Hopefully you'll have corroborating witnesses."

"How can I have witnesses? I'm home every night alone with Lisa! How am I to prove that Tom's lying friends weren't with me?"

TWENTY-ONE

Stephie stood beside the phone without moving. What was happening to her life? How could Tom do this to her? Who would the judge believe? Her or Tom and his three slimy friends?

"Stephie, what did he say?" Paul was at her side.

"Tom's dragging in three friends who'll swear in court that they've slept with me — twice in Lisa's presence." What *Tom* did to her!

"How can they prove such a lie?" Paul countered.

"They don't need to prove it." Stephie's voice cracked. "It's one against four. I won't let him have Lisa!"

"What's your lawyer's plan of action?" He was making an effort to appear calm, but she felt his shock.

"He hopes I'll have witnesses who'll refute Tom's creepy buddies. Witnesses who'll testify that I was with them on the nights they specify." She gave an anguished sigh. "I'm home alone every night in the week — with Lisa. She's four years old — she can't testify!"

"Then your lawyer must find witnesses who'll

place those creeps somewhere else. It won't be easy, but —"

"It won't happen that way!" She dismissed this impatiently. "If we go to court, I'll be made to appear a delinquent mother. Tom will be awarded custody."

"Stephie, you're jumping to the wrong conclusion. The judge will —"

"I won't let Tom get Lisa," she lashed out. "I'll run with her — far from this town. I'll go where he can never find me! Now!"

"We'll go together." All at once the atmosphere was electric. "Emily doesn't need me — she doesn't want me even to phone the kids. We'll go somewhere far away together. You and I and Lisa."

"You'd do that for me?" she whispered.

"For us." Their eyes clung. "We'll drive across the country to Carmel. Create a new life for ourselves. You'll love it there. An endless stretch of beach with steep sand dunes and tall Monterey pines, with rolling hills rising above the beach. Wonderful sunsets. And the town, Stephie —" He pulled her into his arms, willing her to visualise this. "No neon signs are allowed. There's no jail. Only a few sidewalks."

"Paul, do we dare?" Her heart pounded wildly.

"We dare. I knew that someday I'd go back to Carmel. It's a chunk of heaven right here on earth. The two of us together." His voice was reverent. "Together for the rest of our lives."

"I've wanted that so much," she whispered. "I never thought it could happen."

"It was meant to be." It was a glorious benediction. "I can't wait to show you Carmel. Jack London lived there. Robinson Jeffers built himself a stone house atop a cliff looking down on the Pacific and added a miniature medieval tower with a tiny observation post so he could enjoy that magnificent view. John Steinbeck loved Carmel —" He laughed. "I'm running out of breath just trying to describe it for you."

"Tom will never find Lisa there." Her face was luminescent. "Oh, Paul, can we do this?" Could two mere humans enjoy such happiness?

"Can we not do it?" he challenged. "I'll find a teaching job there. We won't live lavishly, but we'll be rich in love and happiness. Our private Eden, Stephie."

"When?" she started.

"Late tonight — when the whole town is asleep."

"I must see Grandma before we leave. I won't tell her," she added quickly. "Not until we're hours out of town. I'll phone her and explain —"

"Stephie, you want to do this?" His eyes searched hers for reassurance.

"More than I've ever wanted anything in my life. For us — and for Lisa."

"I'll drive over for you and Lisa around two A.M.," he plotted. "Then around seven A.M. you'll phone your grandmother from somewhere on the road. You mustn't tell her where we're headed," he cautioned. "Make her understand that's important. But you'll keep in touch." He pressed his face against hers. "Emily told me not to call — she won't be concerned. I'll write her, tell her I won't intrude on her life any longer. She and the boys don't need me — she made that clear."

"I have a little money in the bank. I'll drive down and take most of it out before the bank closes today." Stephie managed a shaky laugh. "I'll be leaving Montauk in high style. In a Mercedes."

Paul stood on the deck and watched Stephie drive away. From the first moment these days in Montauk had been unreal — and wonderful. He felt engulfed in awe. All at once life held new meaning for him. Yet simultaneously he felt a towering sense of loss. He was putting such distance between himself and his sons. But be realistic, he wasn't wanted there.

But Mark was having emotional problems. The school psychologist considered it his parents' fault. With him out of the way Mark wouldn't feel torn between parents because face it, Emily was building up to asking for a divorce. He wasn't the husband she'd expected.

Where had they taken the wrong turn in the road? When she was first pregnant with Mark and suddenly their apartment was inadequate, their income inadequate. He should have insisted they could live without a fancy condo, without an expensive car and all its attendant expenses. They didn't have to worry before Mark was even born about private schools and the prospects of his going to an Ivy League college.

All at once Emily had reverted to wanting the lifestyle she'd known in her growing up years. Years when she had longed for the warmth and love she'd never felt as a child. And he'd let himself be overcome with guilt because he couldn't provide the material things her father had provided.

They'd been on the right path before the kids were born. They — and the kids — could have survived and been happy without the fancy trimmings. But he and Emily got lost. There was so little time, in their race for money, to be with their children.

With him out of the way, Emily would give more of herself to Mark and Larry. She'd feel that was her obligation. The boys would settle down to a stable existence with their mother. No shuttling between parents.

I'll write regularly to Mark and Larry but I won't be a disturbing influence in their lives. They'll know home is with Mommie and accept me as a distant figure who loves them.

With fresh urgency he hurried back into the house. They wouldn't be leaving for hours yet, but he felt a compulsive need to pack. To be ready. He was conscious of a surge of exultation. Stephie and he together for the rest of their lives!

Stephie stopped briefly at the house to pick up her bank passbook and a withdrawal slip. She wouldn't close the account — that might cause curiosity — leave fifty dollars in the account, take out the other few hundred.

Paul wasn't concerned about money. He was sure he'd find a job out there. And once in Carmel he'd be able to sell the car if they needed funds to tide them over. *Thank God, I finished the payments on the car in October; it's mine, free and clear.*

Tom would never know where they'd gone. Nobody would know. Lisa would be safe. Paul would be the father Lisa deserved.

She'd told Paul she'd have no trouble finding a waitress job. Her face glowed with tenderness. He'd said, "I'll work, you'll go back to school. You'll earn that degree in education."

She completed her business at the bank — beautifully decorated for the Christmas season — and headed for the Bertonelli house. Grandma would be there at this hour. She fought for calm while she considered this last encounter with her grandmother until some distant time when they might be together.

Lisa would miss the family Christmas. But as Grandma said, 'Everything in life carries a price tag'. She and Lisa could not be part of the family Christmas reunion but they would be beyond Tom's reach. No way would she allow a judge to grant Tom custody of her precious child.

Stephie waited for her grandmother to respond to the doorbell. She mustn't break down and tell Grandma that she and Lisa were leaving. *Nobody must know until we're well on our way.*

She managed a smile when her grandmother appeared in the foyer.

"I was getting worried," Tina scolded indulgently, opening the door. "I called you three times and didn't get you."

"You didn't leave a message —"

"I hate the damn machines." Tina's frequent complaint. "Come out to the kitchen. I just took panettone out of the oven. You know I like to have it in the house this time of year."

"And you know I can't resist your panettone." *Grandma talks so casually, but her eyes are anxious.*

"I'll give you a chunk to take home to Lisa. It's nice at bedtime. Not too rich."

The kitchen was fragrant with the aroma of fresh baking. Oh, she would miss Grandma, miss the warmth and love that seemed always to permeate this kitchen.

"You know Tom had Lisa for dinner last night, his birthday," she reminded.

"But he brought her back?" Tina was suddenly alert.

"Half an hour past the deadline, but he brought her back. He got nasty — we had a fight. He called me an unfit mother. He threatened to demand full custody."

"He's a big-mouth," Tina dismissed this.

"Stephie, nobody would ever believe that."

"Mr Allen talked to his lawyer. Tom claims I've been having affairs with three men. He's got these three buddies who're ready to go into court and swear I slept with them —" Her voice was unsteady. "He's going into court to ask for full custody."

"We'll show them up as liars." Tina radiated confidence. "I'll swear that I was with you whatever nights those bums claim they were with you. I'll —"

"Grandma, you can't perjure yourself," she interrupted gently. "Those could be nights when you were at some library event or at the Senior Citizens Center or at a church affair."

"I promise you, darling, Tom will never get custody of Lisa. Not even if you and I have to run with her to another country!"

Tears blurred Stephie's vision. "You would do that for us?"

"You're my precious granddaughter. Lisa is my precious great-granddaughter. I would do anything to keep you both safe and happy."

"I'll talk to Mr Allen again," Stephie said. "Ask him what we can do to stop Tom." *I hate lying to Grandma this way.*

"If it's money Tom wants, we'll handle it. Tell that to Mr Allen."

"It's not money anymore. All of a sudden Tom seems to have latched onto an oil well. You saw him in the Land Rover. Mr Allen said he's paid his lawyer. He must have paid off his aunt if she took him back into the house."

"Tell Mr Allen about that," Tina prodded. "Where is Tom getting all that money? It's got a bad smell, Stephie."

"I'll tell him," she promised.

"We won't let Tom ever get custody of Lisa." Tina's face tightened with determination. "You keep remembering that, my darling."

TWENTY-TWO

Stephie climbed behind the wheel of the car. She tried to etch on her mind the image of her grandmother's face when she left the house. *When will I see Grandma again? Will I ever see her again?*

But Paul would be there for her always, she told herself with delicious conviction. Together they'd build a life they were born to live. She and Paul and Lisa — they would be a family.

She'd pack only what she and Lisa would need. Grandma could rent the house furnished as a long seasonal rental. By January the brokers were already receiving calls for summer rentals. The timing was right.

She'd leave a note for Grandma to take care of those missing tiles on the roof, and have Vinnie come over and paint the kitchen ceiling where the leaks showed through. It was a small thing, but she'd never got around to taking care of it.

It was so awful to lie to Grandma. But Paul was right; not even Grandma should know where they were headed. Without meaning to, she might slip up. Tom was so vindictive he'd want to track her down. But he wouldn't find them!

Mom and Dad would be back from Florida the night before Christmas Eve. They would be so upset and angry at her. She'd run off with another man. To them that would be a disgrace for the family. In a little over two years they'd be living in the twenty-first century. Mom and Dad still lived in the nineteenth.

Three times Paul tried to reach the caretaker of the house. Each time he got the answering machine. He'd have to write a note, explaining that he was leaving a few days earlier than planned. Nothing more was necessary. In a desk drawer in the den he found notepaper and envelope, scribbled a brief message. He'd drop it off at the mail box on Main Street when they drove through town. The caretaker would receive it in the morning.

His gear was packed and sat waiting in a corner of the living room. The hours until they were to leave town would seem endless, he warned himself. But it was important to leave in secret, give themselves a head start before those concerned found out Stephie and Lisa were gone — destination unknown.

He prowled about the house, impatient for Stephie to return. They'd have a little while together before she had to pick up Lisa. The rest of the evening must seem routine. She'd take Lisa home. They'd have dinner. She'd prepare Lisa for bed. And at two A.M. he would drive up to their house, carry Lisa — still asleep — out to the car. He and Stephie would pack whatever luggage she was taking with her into the trunk. And then they'd drive away for ever.

He stood at the wall of living room sliders and gazed out onto the sun-drenched ocean. Stephie would be happy at Carmel. She wouldn't have to worry about their being seen together, that Tom would create fresh havoc for her. It would be as though they had been reborn. They were starting their lives anew, the way they were meant to be.

The shrill ring of the phone in the stillness of the house startled him. Frowning, he crossed the room to respond.

"Hello —"

"Paul, it's been awful — I'm so scared!" Emily's voice was shrill with alarm, her words barely coherent. "I'm at Lenox Hill Hospital — Mark's been in an accident!"

"Emily, take a deep breath. Talk slowly. Now tell me what's happened." Despite his outward calm, he was cold with fear.

"A car went out of control, crossed the sidewalk and onto the play area at Mark's school. Oh, Paul. I feel so sick! They couldn't reach me for over an hour! I should have been there for my son!"

"What did the doctors say?" he pushed, his mind in turmoil.

"Mark has a broken arm and a concussion — and we don't know what else." Her voice broke. "I've been such a rotten mother, chasing after a career. We aren't running our lives — our careers are! If anything happens to Mark, I don't deserve to live —"

"Sssh," he ordered. "This accident wasn't your fault. It could have happened to any one of the kids at the school."

"I'm giving notice at the office." Her voice was harsh with self-recrimination. "I'll work part-time, maybe three days a week. No more. I want to be there for Mark and Larry. Paul, we lost our way somewhere —"

Stephie paused at the side door, all at once anxious. Was someone with Paul? Should she leave, come back later? But there was no other car in the driveway; he was on the telephone, she decided in relief. She hurried through the door and down the hall to the living room.

"Emily, he's going to be all right," Paul said, his face drained of color. "I'll be there in about three hours. *Mark's going to be all right.*"

Stephie stood motionless while her mind absorbed Paul's declaration. Something had happened to Mark. Paul was rushing back to New York. Their beautiful dream was over. It was never meant to be.

"Emily, I'll get my gear together and start back. I'll come directly to the hospital. Mark's going to be all right," he repeated yet again. He put down the phone, turned to Stephie.

"You'd better leave right away," she said softly. "And drive carefully." It was God's way of telling them what they were about to do was wrong.

"Some out-of-control car hit Mark," Paul said. "He has a broken arm and a concussion." He took a deep breath. "They don't know what else just yet . . ."

"We had fifteen beautiful days." Her smile was defiant. "Nobody can take those days away from us."

"But you and Lisa —" His face mirrored his anxiety. "How can I —"

"We'll be all right. Like Grandma says, I have a way of over-reacting." She struggled for composure. Their dream was dead. "I'll stay here and we'll work things out. Tom will never gain custody. People here know what he's like. They know his weird friends. Grandma will fight with me. I won't lose custody of Lisa."

"Emily's falling apart —" He gestured his futility. "I have to go back. I have to be there for Mark."

The phone rang. Frowning, Paul reached to pick up the receiver. "Hello?"

"Paul, he's going to be all right!" The caller spoke so loudly in his excitement that Stephie, too, could hear his voice. "Mark has a broken arm and a slight concussion but, thank God, no internal injuries. He'll be home in a couple of days."

"Thanks for letting me know. I'll be heading for New York in a few minutes." His face revealing his inner conflict, Paul put down the phone.

"Mark's going to be all right," Stephie said, and Paul nodded.

"That was my father-in-law. He's at the hospital." Paul's eyes clung to hers, communicating his anguish in silence.

"We must be grateful for what we've had," Stephie whispered. "It was a special Christmas gift that'll be with us forever. Nobody can take it away."

"I'll never go to Carmel," he vowed. "Except in a special corner of my mind that belongs to us alone. Stephie, how am I going to survive without you?"

"We'll have our precious time together to see us through. We've lived more intensely in fifteen days than most people do in their entire lives." One hand moved to caress the pendant Paul had given her. "Part of you will always be with me."

"I thought we'd have the rest of our lives together."

"Let these few days make a wonderful difference," she pleaded. "Don't go back to what you called a jungle. Return to teaching. Make Emily understand —"

"She said, 'Paul, we lost our way somewhere.' I think she does understand." A sense of wonder in his voice. "And promise me, Stephie, you'll find a way to go back to school. To earn a degree in education. Become a teacher. We'll both be giving something to our communities. That's a legacy that'll see us through the years ahead."

They knew not to reach out to touch. Not even for a farewell embrace. The die had been cast. The magic period was over. She searched his face, willing herself to remember him always as he looked at this moment. He would be forever young in her memory. Always a part of her.

I'll always be able to close my eyes and see him again as he is now. He'll always be there for me in a corner of my mind. As I will be for him.

"Goodbye, my love," she whispered and hurried from the room, down the hall and out into the day that had been so beautiful a little while ago.

TWENTY-THREE

Stephie drove away without looking back. She didn't trust herself to look back. Tears blurred her vision as she drove along the empty road. Their dream for tomorrow had fallen prey to reality.

How could Paul walk out on his family? If they'd gone away together, their lives would have been forever haunted by those he'd left behind. And it would have been wrong to deprive Lisa of the richness of her large, loving family. A great-grandmother, grandparents, aunts and uncles and cousins. The Bertonellis shared a closeness that should be cherished. Almost every day Lisa's life was touched by three generations. In the modern world that was a treasure.

Somehow, she would manage to win her divorce from Tom. Somehow, she would make sure Tom never received even shared custody. Lisa would be surrounded by love. She owed that to her daughter.

She brushed away the tears, drove without destination. She and Paul would be separated by many miles, but in their hearts they would relive every wonderful moment. She would remember forever the way his eyes followed her every movement when they were in a room together, as though he couldn't bear an instant's separation.

Throughout the years, in every rough period — and these were bound to happen — she'd remember the fifteen magical days here in Montauk when Paul was with her. *And the memory will give me the strength to carry on.*

With a sudden compulsion to see her grandmother she drove now with a destination in mind. Only Grandma knew about Paul and her. Tom had never known. It was her rejection of him and his jealousy of Gary that had motivated his insane demands. Grandma had such wisdom. Grandma would help her in her fight against Tom.

She parked in the driveway, relieved to hear the sound of the radio, which told her Grandma was home. The front door was unlocked. She walked inside.

"Grandma —" All at once she was conscious of a tidal wave of desolation. Two hours ago the world had seemed such a beautiful place because she and Paul, along with Lisa, would soon be on their way to a whole new life. "Grandma?" Alarm closed in about her.

"I'll be down in a minute," Tina called from upstairs. "I'm in my sewing room."

Stephie waited at the foot of the stairs, her heart pounding. She must focus on defeating Tom in his latest craziness. *No way will I allow him to have custody of Lisa!*

"I've been making this little nightie for Lisa." Tina was coming down the stairs. "I saw a picture in a magazine, and I know she'll love it." She stopped dead. "Something's happened —"

"Lisa's fine. I'm all right." She took a deep breath. "Paul's leaving Montauk."

"Darling, you knew that was bound to happen."

"We almost made a terrible mistake."

In total candor Stephie told her grandmother about the love she and Paul had shared, about their plan to cross the country to build a secret new life for themselves. And then she told her about Mark's accident.

"We both realized it wasn't meant to be. Paul must rebuild his life with his family and Lisa and I would be the poorer without our family. But I know I'll love him forever, and he feels the same about me. Our timing was all wrong."

"Something precious came into your life, Stephie." Tina reached for Stephie's hand, walked with her into the living room. "Sit down, my darling, and let me tell you something nobody in this world knows except me and your grandfather." She paused, her face lit with a special inner light. "You see, the man you knew as your grandfather — the man Tony knew as his father — was that in name only. Your grandfather was that American GI that I've talked about so often."

"Oh, Grandma —" She'd always suspected

211

Grandma had been in love with him.

"Steve was billeted in our house for four months. Almost immediately we fell in love. Those were desperate times. You'd have to live through a war to understand. We never knew when his company would move ahead. We never knew if he would survive the war. But I knew that he had a wife and a toddler son back home. There was no tomorrow for us but we clung to the moment. Then suddenly it was VE Day, and his company was to be shipped home. We knew we could never see each other again. He didn't know I was pregnant."

"You never told him?"

"There could be no future for us. Tony knew I was pregnant — I couldn't lie to him. But he wanted to marry me anyway. Nobody else ever realized your father was a full-term baby. We said he came two months early. Tony was a good father to all my sons. He was a fine grandfather to you and the boys."

"You named me for your American GI," Stephie whispered, suffused with love. "My grandfather."

"From the day you were born, you were the image of him. I told Tony and your mother — she'll be named Stephie. That's one of the reasons you — and Lisa, who looks exactly like you — are especially precious to me. You don't just look like Steve. You have his little mannerisms, the way of tilting your head to one side when you're deep in thought — oh, in so many little ways, my darling."

"You've never forgotten him." As she would never forget Paul.

"Part of Steve has always been with me. And it'll be the same for you."

"Will I survive this?" Anguish seemed to stifle her. "Will I be strong, the way you've been strong?"

Tina pulled her close. "You'll survive my darling, and for ever be a richer person for having known him. You've shared a little taste of heaven that you'll cherish the rest of your life." An inner glow lit her face. "Even now, all these years later, I can close my eyes and see Steve, the way he was all those years ago. I feel so close to him. You'll be fine, Stephie," she said resolutely.

"I want to go college and earn a degree in education. Paul said I should do that. All my life I've wanted to be a teacher. I can do that and still be a good mother. Grandma, can I come back home and go to college? With summer school I can make it in three years. Will you help me?"

"I should have sent you to college when you finished high school but I was scared you'd get your education and move away from us. I let your mother and father persuade me that they needed you in the restaurant, that your future lay there. I suspect that Gary will be proud to have a wife who's a teacher," she said tenderly. "And there's no reason you can't be married and go to college at the same time."

"Grandma, I still have to get my divorce —"

213

"That'll happen." Tina was grim. "And no question of Tom's ever having custody."

"From your lips to God's ear," Stephie whispered, fighting tears.

"I talk to God about this regularly," Tina said, her smile dazzling.

"Tina!" a woman's excited voice called from the porch. "Tina, are you home?"

"The door's open —" Tina rose to her feet. "Come on in, Jane."

"I can't believe what I just heard —" A small, round woman in her fifties hurried into the house. She stopped short at the sight of Stephie. "Oh, Stephie . . ." She seemed hesitant now.

"Jane, what's got you so upset?" Tina clucked.

"Well, not exactly upset . . ." She paused, gazed at Stephie. "You're almost divorced from Tom, so I suppose I can say it —"

"Jane, spill it," Tina ordered. "What's happened?"

"It's about Tom. He's in jail down in Riverhead. He's been caught selling hard drugs."

"Oh, Alice must be so upset." Tina was instantly compassionate.

"I wouldn't say so. It was Alice who tipped off the police. She realized Tom was using her house to stash heroin. Using her phone to conduct his business. And not only was he dealing drugs, he roughed up a couple down there who were delinquent in their payments. You know Alice — she may be odd sometimes, but she's as law-abiding as they come."

"He'll be put away for years." Tina was serene. "You'll get your divorce, Stephie. And no court on this earth will award custody of a child to a felon."

"I have to get back home — I have family coming for dinner tonight. But I figured you'd want to know." Jane gazed uncertainly from Tina to Stephie.

"Thank you for telling us," Stephie said. "We wanted to know."

Stephie and Tina went out to the kitchen to sit down over coffee and Tina's perfect panettone.

"I'll have to leave soon to pick up Lisa," Stephie reminded.

"And sometime this evening, when the word gets around about Tom, I suspect you'll be hearing from Gary. Your life will come together, I promise you. And you're a lucky woman, Stephie. You may have had a rotten husband, but two fine men love you."